PRAISE FOR
The
allegra biscotti
Collection

"Credible characterizations and dialogue keep the novel real. For *Project Runway* aspirants, Bennett slips in detailed descriptions of the teens' outfits and Emma's designs, which appear in spot art."

—*Publishers Weekly*

"This book manages to make the wildly implausible seem possible...Emma, Marjorie, and Charlie are well rounded...Kids interested in fashion are sure to become fans of *The Allegra Biscotti Collection*."

—Tina Zubak, Carnegie Library of Pittsburgh,
School Library Journal

"This book speaks to the teenager hidden somewhere in me that still wants to be discovered and be a star. This story is exactly like a thousand fantasies I've had myself, and so I could do nothing but love it, love it, love it."

—Jackie Blem, Tattered Cover

"*The Allegra Biscotti Collection* by Olivia Bennett, ages 9–11, is about a fourteen-year-old who becomes a fashion designer; Coco Chanel step aside! The voice is perfect for projecting the personality of the main characters. I especially liked the personalities of the Ivana-Bees! I remember those girls in school!"

—Judith Lafitte, Octavia Books

"I love books like *Allegra Biscotti* and I think the packaging for this book is great. It looks contemporary, a little but not too grown up—I think of it as the twixt and tween reader that grows up to read Candace Bushnell. The story seems real and the dialogue is chatty, crisp, really believable. Thanks for sharing with me, and I'd love to see more!"

—Vicki Erwin, Main Street Books

"I love the packaging! It looks great, and I look forward to reading it and maybe passing it on to my youngest daughter!"

—Stephanie Kilgore, Changing Hands

"The wild adventures of Emma Rose will keep readers laughing. Young fashionistas will appreciate Emma's keen eye for style, and might even inspire girls to try their own hand at design. *Allegra Biscotti* is a must for all tween collections."

— Rita Reale, Children's Librarian, *The Cats Meow*
(Baker & Taylor Newsletter)

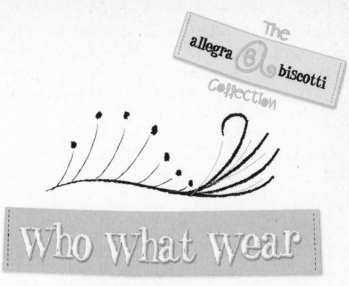

The allegra B biscotti collection

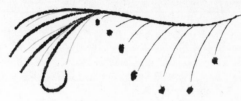

who what wear

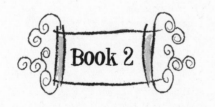

Book 2

OLIVIA BENNETT
ILLUSTRATED BY GEORGIA RUCKER

sourcebooks
jabberwocky

Published by Sourcebooks Jabberwocky, an imprint of Sourcebooks, Inc.
P.O. Box 4410, Naperville, Illinois 60567-4410
(630) 961-3900
Fax: (630) 961-2168
www.jabberwockykids.com

Library of Congress Cataloging-in-Publication data is on file with the publisher.

Source of Production: Versa Press, East Peoria, Illinois, USA.
Date of Production: April 2011
Run Number: 15011

Printed and bound in the United States of America.
VP 10 9 8 7 6 5 4 3 2 1

With special thanks
to Catherine Hapka

"In order to be irreplaceable,
one must always be different."

—*Coco Chanel*

CHAPTER 1

FASHIONABLY GREAT

Emma Rose dug through the pile of clothing. Soft, caramel-colored herringbone wool pants. Plum, cap-sleeved, silk cocktail dress. Camel, V-neck cashmere sweater. Totally luxe, but totally boring.

Then her hand closed on something different.

"Hey, what's this?" she asked, as she pulled out a child-sized dress made from cupcake-pink velvet with a smocked front and a full skirt.

"My sixth-birthday party dress!" Holly Richardson cried. "I can't believe my mother kept it this long! Do you remember how much I loved this thing?"

"Yeah. Now I recognize it! You wore it every chance you got, even after your mom threatened to throw it into the East River." Emma grinned. "I think I still have some old photos of you in it. Remember that freak warm spell that winter, when my dad took us to the park? We ran around with our coats off blowing bubbles and chasing pigeons."

Holly clapped her hands. "I remember that day! Your dad bought us those huge swirly lollipops after we begged and begged for them, and we both ended up with stomachaches."

"That was an amazing day. Stomachaches and all." Emma ran her fingers over the smocking, a little stiff with age but still impeccably crafted. "She kept this for a long time," she commented. "Why's your mom getting rid of it now?"

"Who knows?" Holly shrugged. "Probably it got put away somewhere in the back of a closet, and she just found it. You know she's not exactly sentimental about stuff like that. She tosses everything."

"Yeah, so not like my mom. She still has every single one of my baby teeth. My brother's, too."

"Seriously?" Holly wrinkled her nose. "Gross!"

"I know." Holding the dress up, Emma checked her reflection in the gilded, ornate mirror in the foyer of her best friend's Manhattan apartment. "If I recut this and maybe combined it with, like, a soft plaid flannel or something, I could turn it into a totally cool minidress," she mused, mentally sketching out the possibilities.

Holly looked impressed. "You're amazing, Em. I mean, I know I tell you that all the time, but it's true. You will totally be a famous fashion designer. You know, someday."

Emma's heart skipped a beat, and she shot her friend a nervous look. Did Holly know? Could she have found out somehow?

But no. Holly's face remained open and cheerful as she chewed her gum and poked through the pile of clothes, and Emma relaxed. Her best friend still didn't know the most incredibly, amazingly, unbelievably fabulous secret Emma had ever had.

She was Allegra Biscotti.

Emma still shivered every time she thought about it, hardly daring to believe it was true. She was a real, honest-to-goodness fashion designer! Her clothes had been featured on the hottest fashion blog, StylePaige, and would be appearing in an upcoming issue of *Madison* magazine. Having to keep a secret like that from Holly—especially today, when they were having such a great time going through the clothes Mrs. Richardson was donating to charity—was pretty much a huge bummer.

Emma couldn't do much about it, though. She'd been sworn to secrecy by none other than Paige Young, the senior fashion editor at *Madison* who'd discovered Allegra Biscotti. Of course, Paige *hadn't* discovered Emma was only fourteen until after she'd already featured Emma's clothes on her StylePaige blog. Emma knew that Paige's career—not to mention her own—probably depended on keeping Allegra's true identity as well hidden as a society lady's Spanx. Still, she wondered, what harm would it do to tell her best friend?

"You know," Holly said as she grabbed a lavender pashmina out of the clothing pile and threw it over her shoulders, "I'm pretty sure Ivana's dad represents some fashion designers and stuff at his law firm. Maybe she could hook you up. You know, help you meet the right people to get started."

Emma's urge to share her secret popped like one of Holly's fruity-scented bubble-gum bubbles. Somehow, she'd almost forgotten one very important fact. These days, Holly told Ivana Abbott *everything*.

Emma reached into the nearest box and pulled out a full-length bathrobe in a garish floral silk. "Here's where I show my true design talents," she joked, slipping into the robe and tying it off with a jaunty bow at one hip. "This will be all the rage in Milan next spring."

"Wait, you need the finishing touch." Grabbing a wide, purple leather belt from the pile, Holly wrapped it around Emma's upper torso like a bustier. "There!" She put her fingers to her lips and made a dramatic kissing gesture. "Delicious!"

Emma giggled, glancing at her reflection. She looked ridiculous! She piled her shoulder-length brown hair high on her head and used one of the hair bands from around her wrist to secure it in a very messy twist. Adopting a pouty expression, she stalked across the living room, adding an exaggerated model's twirl at the far end, while Holly collapsed on the sofa with laughter.

"Eet eez zee next beeg theeng!" Emma cried in a cartoonish French accent. "Zee height of fashion!"

"Really? Nobody told me tacky and hideous were back in style."

Emma froze. That wasn't Holly's voice.

She spun around. Holly's older sister, Jennifer, and two of her super-fabulous high-school friends stood in the doorway staring at her. Emma's face flamed, and she quickly yanked off the purple belt and tossed it back into the pile of clothes. "We, um, were just goofing around," she muttered.

She couldn't quite meet the gaze of the girl who'd spoken, though she found herself admiring the girl's outfit out of the corner of her eye. Sleek, black skinny jeans; a silver quilted, fitted jacket; and a black nylon hobo bag with a tomato-red lining. Fabulous.

Emma doubted the girl knew her name, though Emma certainly knew hers. *Everyone* did. Jennifer and all of her friends were popular, but Rylan Sinclare was pretty much on a different plane. It wasn't that Rylan was especially beautiful or smart or talented. In fact, she was sort of ordinary looking, with a square face, long nose, and eyes set a little too close together.

But she was tall and slim and had an air about her, a certain self-confident vibe that exuded from the top of her chin-length, chestnut-brown bob to the tips of her designer shoes (quilted, red suede ballet flats on this particular day), that made everyone pay attention whenever she walked into the room.

"Playing dress-up is so second grade," the third girl said with a sniff. Val Capolla was petite with short dreads and a winter-white flared trench coat with chocolate-brown piping and a square, brown suede belt buckle.

"What are you doing here, Jen?" Holly demanded as Emma peeled off the silk robe, feeling about as sophisticated as that little girl who'd eaten lollipops in the park all those years ago. "I thought you were going to the movies."

"So sorry I didn't have my social secretary notify you about our change of plans." Jennifer was tall, blond, and gorgeous—pretty much Holly plus two years and a lot of attitude, at least when her snooty friends were around.

"Whatev." Holly glared at her older sister. "I was just asking. It's not like I—"

The *Project Runway* elimination jingle cut off Holly's train of thought.

"That's me." Rylan fished a sleek silver cell out of a fold in the red lining of her bag. "It's my mother," she announced after glancing at the phone.

Val widened her perfectly lined brown eyes. "Are you going to answer?"

"Are you certifiable?" Rylan stuck the phone back in her bag.

But a few seconds later, the ringtone blared again. "Your mom?" Jennifer asked.

Rylan checked the caller ID. "Uh-huh." She shot her friends a wicked smirk. "Guess this means she found the dress."

Jennifer and Val laughed loudly. "Come on, let's grab those cookies you said you have," Val said. "I can't eat that dreck they sell at the theater. Makes me break out."

The older girls wandered off toward the kitchen without another glance at Emma and Holly. "Well, that was fun," Holly commented. "Jen is so lame when she's around her stuck-up friends."

"Yeah, I know. Totally Jekyll and Hyde." Emma started picking up the clothes she and Holly had strewn around and tossing them back into their boxes. She heard Rylan's ringtone again, fainter now but still loud enough to carry

7

throughout the apartment. "I wonder what Rylan meant about her mother finding a dress."

"It's always about the clothes with you, isn't it?" Holly teased. Then she shrugged. "Probably something to do with her Sweet Sixteen."

"Is she having a party?"

"More than that!" Holly's blue eyes lit up. "Jen says it's going to be insane! People over at the high school are already going nuts trying to make sure they're invited, even though nobody even knows when or where it's going to be yet. Not even Jen and the rest of Rylan's friends. Totally top secret! Isn't that crazy cool?"

"Hmm." Emma wasn't sure what else to say. She had more important things on her mind these days than some snobby high-school party. Like setting up an official website for Allegra Biscotti. Sketching and imagining her next designs just in case the *Madison* feature led to something else… but really because she couldn't *not* think about designing. Wondering and worrying whether Allegra's overnight success had been a fluke…

But Holly seemed fascinated, so Emma tried to look interested. That was what friends did. Right?

Jennifer, Rylan, and Val sauntered back into the living room, heading toward the front door. "You're still here?" Jennifer quipped when she spotted Emma and Holly. Emma winced. She could remember all those afternoons when they were little and Jen would play Polly Pockets with her and Holly, giggling and acting totally silly. That Jen was obviously long gone.

Rylan laughed. "Why are you surprised?" she said. "Where else do you think *they* have to go? Especially dressed like that." Then her phone rang again deep inside her bag.

"Turn that thing off already, will you?" Jennifer complained. "I don't want to listen to it all through the movie."

"Yeah, good call." Rylan reached in and clicked a button on the phone. "You know my mother. She's relentless."

All three girls laughed as they hurried out. Emma was glad to see them go. Most kids at Downtown Day School admired Rylan and wanted to be around her. But as far as Emma was concerned, Rylan was just an older, slightly better dressed and even more obnoxious version of Ivana. What did otherwise sane people like Holly and Jennifer see in girls like that, anyway?

She jumped at the familiar chirping of Holly's ringtone. Holly pounced on a pile of clothes, digging through it until she found her phone. She glanced at the caller ID, then grinned and pressed the phone to her ear.

"Ivana? What's up, girl?" she exclaimed.

Emma's heart sank. She should have known

her fun Saturday afternoon with Holly was too good to be true. It had been like this since school started this year. Not bothering to listen as Holly chattered cheerfully into the phone, Emma wandered out into the kitchen to grab a bottle of water out of the fridge.

"Call you back in a sec," Holly said as Emma came back into the living room. "Bye." She clicked off the phone and glanced over. "That was Ivana."

"Yeah, I heard." Emma twisted the cap off the water bottle. "I thought she had some kind of family thing today."

"Canceled." Holly smiled hopefully. "She just invited us to come meet her and the girls at Narcissia."

"Us?" Emma echoed. "Or you?"

Holly blew a purple bubble and popped it. "What's the diff?" she asked. "I told her you and I are hanging out today, so she knows we come as a set. Anyway, they're trying to help Lexie pick out something new to wear when she hangs out with Jackson tonight."

Emma winced. Lexie Blackburn was one of Ivana's three BFFs-slash-admirers, collectively known as the Ivana-Bees, as in "I Wanna Be Ivana." Jackson Creedon was the new boy in school and pretty much Emma's dream guy. Put Jackson and the Ivana-Bees together, and what did you have? Basically, Emma's worst nightmare.

Holly caught her eye, looking sympathetic. "Sorry. But

look, you'd definitely be able to help her find a perfect outfit. I also totally understand if you don't want to help Lexie look hot for Jackson. If you don't want to go, I'll tell Ivana we can't make it."

Was Holly really willing to pass up an afternoon with Ivana and the Bees for her? This was serious progress. Maybe things weren't as weird between them as she'd thought. Maybe all those years of being best friends still counted.

She eyed Holly and immediately knew. Holly was really hoping she'd say yes. Emma had seen that look so many times before. "You go," she said instead. "I need to head home anyway. I'm technically still grounded, remember?"

"Oh right, I forgot. We were supposed to be studying for that world history test, weren't we?" Holly grinned. "Oops!"

"Yeah. So have fun shopping and I'll talk to you later, okay?"

"Okay, if you're sure."

"I'm sure." Emma reached for the pink, smocked child's dress. "Think your mom would mind if I took this?"

"Are you kidding? She won't even notice. Take it." Holly smiled. "I'll text you later."

Moments later, as Emma walked down the hushed, carpeted hallway of Holly's apartment building, she replayed what had just happened. Holly had seemed sincerely willing to turn down Ivana's invitation if Emma wanted. But she hadn't exactly tried to change Emma's mind when she'd offered to leave either. So who did Holly like better? Emma or Ivana? It was hard to tell.

Once inside the elevator, Emma tucked the child's dress into her black canvas messenger bag, which she had decorated in zebra stripes with a silver Sharpie, and pulled out a sketchbook. By the time the doors slid open in the lobby, she had the sweet, pink dress halfway redesigned into a chic, modern mini. Her feet automatically carried her down the sidewalk of Holly's tree-lined Upper East Side street toward the nearest subway station. She pulled out her cell phone and dialed.

"Yo," Charlie Calhoun's familiar voice answered on the second ring.

"Hi," Emma said. "What's up? Are you working on the site?"

"I've been slaving away all day. The people at Tome probably think I've moved in permanently."

Emma smiled, picturing him sitting at one of the rickety, mismatched tables in their favorite funky little hole-in-the-wall independent bookstore, creating a website for Allegra Biscotti. "Thanks for doing this. You know computer stuff puts me to sleep even faster than math class."

"You stick to the fashion, and I'll take care of the tech."

"Sounds like a plan. I—" Emma stopped short as she heard a strange buzzing from inside her bag. What was that? The buzz sounded again, and suddenly the answer hit her. "Oops, hold on a sec," she told Charlie, jamming her cell between her cheek and her shoulder as she reached into her bag. "The Allegra phone's ringing."

The new website wasn't the only new requirement from Paige. She also wanted Emma to have a separate phone just for Allegra's calls. Yesterday after school Emma and Charlie had picked out a sleek cherry-colored flip phone that seemed perfect for Allegra. This was the first time it had rung. She would definitely have to find a new ringtone!

"Hold on, hold on," she muttered as she dug deeper into her bag, searching for the phone as it buzzed again. "Where are you?"

"What?" Charlie's voice drifted into her ear.

"Not talking to you." Emma twisted her head around, trying not to drop her own phone as she searched for the other. Why hadn't she put Allegra's phone in the little pouch where she kept hers?

No, forget that. She knew the answer. Allegra was a secret. How was she supposed to explain having two cell phones if someone like Holly noticed?

"Hey! Watch it!"

Emma glanced up just in time to avoid running into a pair of nannies pushing matching double strollers. "Um, sorry," she mumbled, darting around the strollers while four sets of wide baby eyes stared at her with fascination.

The Allegra phone kept buzz, buzz, buzzing! Who was on the phone? Could she be missing the biggest fashion opportunity of her career?

Emma frantically yanked her world history textbook out of the bag and dropped it to the sidewalk at her feet. It crashed against the concrete, sounding like a gunshot and causing at least two of the babies that had just passed to wail.

The nannies threw Emma dirty looks as they pushed the strollers away faster.

"I just remembered," Charlie shouted through the phone she still held awkwardly to her ear by her shoulder. "I never set the Allegra phone to voice mail."

"Yeah, I kind of figured that out after the eleventh ring," Emma said. "I'm calling you back." She shoved her phone in the fleece-lined pocket of her vintage faux-leopard coat. The coat had been one of her favorite thrift-shop finds. The *perfect* leopard print, a body-skimming cut, and just-right mid-thigh length. But Emma was always freezing, so she had found an old powder-blue fleece and used it to line the body to make it winter warm. She'd used the extra fleece to line the pockets—one of which was now keeping the Charlie phone warm while she searched for her other cell.

She pulled more stuff out of her bag. The pink smocked dress. Her sketchbook. Some jewel-toned fabric scraps she'd rescued from the free bin at her favorite fabric shop, Allure. A half-finished set of math problems. An interesting brocade fan she'd picked up in Chinatown. A handful of rhinestone pins shaped like bugs. Suddenly all Holly's teasing about Emma keeping her whole life in the messenger bag didn't seem so funny—or make Emma feel so professional.

Finally her hand closed on the cool metal of Allegra's phone. She snatched it from the bottom of the bag. "Hello?" she said breathlessly, as a young boy glided by on a skateboard, staring curiously at the pile of random stuff at her feet. "Uh, Allegra Biscotti's office?"

"Emma?" a voice barked out. "That you?"

Emma gulped, feeling a familiar rush of nerves. "Hi, Paige. Yes, it's me. So you got the new phone number I texted you, huh? That's good. I—"

"Listen, I don't have much time—I'm already five minutes late for a production meeting," Paige interrupted, talking at warp speed. "But I wanted to touch base with you before I go in. You probably already heard that *Madison* is going to be sponsoring a totally exclusive pop-up shop here in the city next month, right?"

"Um, no?" Emma felt slightly stupid. Sometimes Paige seemed to forget she was only fourteen and still fairly new to the fashion world.

"It's going to be huge, huge, huge," Paige said. "The shop will only be open for one weekend—and will only feature clothing from up-and-coming designers." She barked out a laugh. "The press is already eating it up."

"Sounds cool." Emma wasn't sure why Paige was in a rush to tell her all this if she was running so late. She could hear the echo of Paige's stilettos click-clacking double-time down a hallway.

Emma's bag suddenly slipped off her shoulder, and she automatically grabbed at it, almost dropping the phone. Catching it just in time, she shifted it to her other ear and missed part of whatever Paige said next.

"…schedule is tight, and there isn't a minute to lose, but it'll all be worth it," Paige was saying. "This is going to be huge for Allegra! As in gigantic! No, bigger than that!"

Emma stared blindly out at the traffic passing on Lexington Avenue as she tried to follow what Paige was saying. "Um, what is?" she asked tentatively.

"Are you deaf?" Paige sounded impatient. "My boss just agreed that Allegra Biscotti's holiday line is going to be featured in our Choice New Designers pop-up shop. You'll be one of the ten designers featured. This is it, Emma. Make-it-or-break-it time for Allegra Biscotti. You're going to be a star!"

CHAPTER 2

WHO'S WHO AND WHAT'S WHAT

Emma was still absorbing the details of her conversation with Paige. She'd have to come up with six items to hang on the Allegra Biscotti rack at the *Madison* pop-up shop. Her mind was already spinning with possibilities when she reached the heavy wooden door to Tome.

"You're not going to believe this!" Emma cried as she squeezed into the cramped seating area in the back of the store where Charlie was holed up. "Allegra's going to be a star!"

Charlie sat at a wobbly old library table in the corner. He'd been bent over his laptop, but he spun around at the sound of her voice. Propped atop his head, half-hidden in his spiky white-blond hair, was a pair of mirrored wraparounds straight out of a cheesy eighties music video. He had tons of shades and wore a different pair every day. The rest of his outfit stuck closer to the current century. Worn-out Levi's and a kung-fu tee over a long-sleeved waffle thermal. "Huh?" he said.

"I just talked to Paige," Emma said, slinging her messenger

bag onto the table, which shivered in protest 〔
going to believe what she told me!"

"Yeah, you mentioned that." Charlie rea⟨
energy-drink can by his elbow and took a swig. "Allegr⟨
going to be a star. So what else is new?"

Emma grabbed a chair and flopped down onto it, sending
up a puff of dust that made her sneeze. "No, listen, I'm
serious! This is big news. *Madison* magazine is doing
a pop-up shop next month," she began.

"A pop-what what? Is that one of your weird
fashion terms?"

"It means a temporary store where they can show
off new designs to important store buyers and get
publicity and stuff." Emma leaned forward. "This
one's going to be in this totally cool old building in
SoHo. It'll only be open for one weekend."

"Oh." Charlie's gaze was already wandering back
to his laptop. "So this is a shopping thing. Listen,
which font do you think we should use for the—"

"Charlie!" Emma leaned across the table, grabbed
his shoulders, and shook him. "Focus, okay? It's not
a shopping thing. It's an Allegra thing. Paige just told
me that Allegra Biscotti is going to be one of only
ten new designers featured in their totally exclusive
pop-up shop!"

What?" That got Charlie's attention. "Hold on. You mean your clothes are going to be in some fancy, big-time *Madison* thingy?"

Emma grinned. "Yeah. Some fancy, big-time *Madison* thingy that's going to be covered in every fashion magazine from here to Tokyo!"

Charlie leaped to his feet so fast he almost knocked over his drink. "Spectacular!" His voice echoed through the quiet store. "Emma, that's amazing! Happy dance!"

He stood up and started wiggling his legs and flapping his arms. Emma giggled and joined in, tossing both hands over her head and shimmying her hips. An old man at the next table peered at them over the tops of his bifocals and smiled while a college-aged girl looked at them like they were crazy.

"Everything okay back here, kids?"

Emma looked over her shoulder. Mr. Baum, the owner of the bookshop, peeked at them over a tall stack of oversized art books. He was dressed in his usual uniform of baggy khakis and a message T-shirt. Today the message was: "Question Authority."

"Sorry, Mr. B," Charlie said. "Um, we were just leaving."

Soon the two of them were perched on a bench in a tiny

neighborhood park. Several teenage boys played basketball nearby. Emma barely noticed them as she repeated everything Paige had told her. Charlie had told her not to leave out one word.

"The shop will showcase small collections by new designers," she said.

"Which ones?" Charlie asked. "Besides you, I mean."

"Not sure. Paige was in kind of a hurry, so I didn't get all the details." Emma bit her lip. Paige always flustered her. She could never think straight when she was talking with the fashion editor. Suddenly, Emma realized that maybe she should have asked some questions. Or maybe not. With Paige, it was hard to know. "She'll probably write about it on her blog. But I do know I'll need to create some holiday looks—fast."

"You can do it." Charlie didn't sound worried at all. "Paige must think so, too, or she wouldn't have talked them into including you. And she's a pro, right? She knows nobody's hotter than Allegra Biscotti. You can tell just by looking at Allegra's hot new website."

"I almost forgot. How's that going?"

"See for yourself." Charlie pulled his laptop out of his bag, flipped it open, and hit a key.

Emma had chosen colors, borders, and fonts the previous afternoon, but she had left the rest up to Charlie. She couldn't believe what he'd done.

"Do you like it?" Charlie sounded uncharacteristically uncertain for a second.

"Are you kidding? I love it!" Emma leaned closer for a better look. "Oh wow, is that my wall?"

She pointed to a photo image that formed the background of the navigation box on the left-hand side of the home page. It showed her inspiration wall, the eight-foot-high space above the worktable in her studio. The wall was an ever-changing mosaic of interesting images and ideas—magazine clippings, fabric swatches, photos of outrageous outfits, and sketches of new ideas.

And that wasn't all. Charlie had incorporated a bunch of other images onto the home page, too. Photos of Allegra's clothes. Some of Emma's latest sketches. And more. It was a busy, funky design that somehow managed to be cool and fun at the same time.

"Allegra's bio is here." Charlie hit a link. "I fiddled with it a little. See what you think. Once we nail that down, we'll be almost ready to go live."

Emma scanned the bio, which she and Charlie had written during study hall the day before. They'd invented an entire backstory for Allegra Biscotti—born in Milan, designed her first dress at age eight, traveled the world doing exotic things and having exciting adventures—

"Wait a sec," Emma said. "I don't remember this part about Allegra working as a bullfighter in Spain."

Charlie grinned. "Brilliant, right?"

"Bullfighting seems kind of, you know, mean to the bulls," Emma said. "Plus, Allegra doesn't have time for stuff like that. She's all about the clothes. And bullfighters' uniforms are all gold-braid this, red-cape that. Kind of tacky."

"Aw, come on. Where's your spirit of adventure?"

"Not in the bull pen."

Charlie shrugged and obeyed, deleting the reference and quickly cleaning up the spacing. "There," he said. "Happy now?"

"Ecstatic." Emma was already scanning the list of links. She recognized most of them: *Madison*'s home page, Paige's style blog, and various other fashion sites. "Hold on," she said. "What's the American Society for Extraterrestrial Communication?"

"Just what it sounds like. They have a really cool site. Thought it made ours seem more compelling."

Emma laughed. *Compelling* was such a Charlie Calhoun word. "Sorry, got to veto that one, too," she said. "Besides, I don't think Paige will go for it."

"Who's in charge here? Paige or Allegra?" Charlie protested.

"Well…Allegra doesn't like it either."

Emma's silver sneakers carried her up the steps and through the front doors of Downtown Day on autopilot Monday morning. Her only focus was on getting to her locker so she could get her latest idea down on paper.

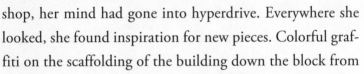

Emma's mind was always teeming with design ideas. But since finding out about the pop-up shop, her mind had gone into hyperdrive. Everywhere she looked, she found inspiration for new pieces. Colorful graffiti on the scaffolding of the building down the block from her. A subway rider's handmade patchwork bag. These totally cool European tourists, two girls probably in their twenties, wearing super-short smock dresses with colored fishnets *over* tights and puffy down vests.

"Hi, Em!"

Emma glanced up and saw Holly waving to her from their side by side lockers. That normally wouldn't be a problem. Even though Holly didn't know about Allegra, she was used to Emma's fashion obsession and wouldn't think twice if Emma grabbed her sketchbook and started drawing before she even said, "Good morning."

The problem was that Holly wasn't alone. Ivana was there, too.

Of course.

Emma wanted to stop, to run away somewhere private where she could sketch without risking any snooty comments from Ivana and her friends. But it was too late. She was only a few feet away, and they'd seen her already.

"Em, you totally should have come to Narcissia the other day!" Holly exclaimed, snapping her gum. Double strawberry today, by the smell of it. "Lexie must have tried on every outfit in the store."

"Some of them twice." Ivana leaned against the wall of lockers, playing with the bluntly trimmed ends of her flat-ironed auburn hair.

"Oh." Emma wasn't sure how they expected her to respond. She felt that way a lot when Ivana and the Bees were around.

Or even Ivana and *some* of her Bees. Lexie wasn't there, but Kayla Levine and Shannon O'Malley were in close orbit around Planet Ivana, as usual.

"Totally." Kayla blinked at Emma. Her lashes were so thickly coated in indigo-colored mascara that Emma was surprised she could move them. Kayla's mother had started her own cosmetics company called Beautylicious, and Kayla liked to advertise the entire product line on her own face. Usually all at once.

"But it was worth it," Shannon reminded the others, tugging self-consciously at the hem of her way-too-short skirt, a black mini that Emma was fairly sure she'd borrowed from Ivana. "She ended up with a totally cute outfit."

Emma wasn't biting. She didn't want to hear about the cute outfit that Lexie wore to impress Jackson.

"Hmm." Emma bent over to open her locker so the others wouldn't see her expression. All of these girls spent serious money on their clothes but never really wore anything interesting. It never seemed to occur to them that they were actually allowed to put together outfits that *didn't* come straight out of a display window or a catalog.

Emma's outfit didn't cost very much, but it was creative and totally Emma. Over super-comfortable, worn-out, and slightly stretchy jeans, she wore a long-sleeved red cotton jersey T-shirt under a striped sweater-vest that had been her father's pullover before it was destroyed by moths in his closet. Emma had simply washed and machine-dried it to shrink it and then cut off the moth-eaten sleeves. She loved that it was still a bit roomy and frayed around the sleeves where she'd cut them.

By the time Emma straightened up again, Ivana was staring off down the hall. "Here she comes," she announced.

Following her gaze, Emma saw Lexie slinking down the hall in jeans that were so tight they could have been tights, wearing Jackson on her arm like the latest designer accessory.

"Shh," Holly said with a giggle. "We don't want Jackson to know we spent hours helping her shop for their date."

Thanks, DAD

"What up, girls?" Lexie said when she reached them. "Did you hear the news?"

"What news?" Ivana squinted suspiciously at Lexie. She liked to be the first one in school to know everything.

Lexie tossed her smooth, almost-black hair over one shoulder. As she did, she released Jackson's arm. He slouched over and leaned against the locker next to Emma's.

"Hey," he muttered, nodding to Emma.

Emma's throat suddenly went dry. "Um, hey," she mumbled.

She was only vaguely aware that Lexie was talking again. Something about blah-blah-blah Rylan Sinclare's Sweet Sixteen party blah-blah-blah. Emma didn't catch the details, and she didn't really care. She was way too aware of Jackson standing there. Was he looking at her with those deep blue eyes of his? She didn't dare glance over to find out.

Then she snapped out of it—a little, at least—when Holly

let out an ear-piercing squeal. "OMG!" Holly cried. "Emma and I totally ran into Rylan over the weekend. She was in my apartment!"

"Whoa, really?" Kayla sounded impressed, and Shannon's eyes widened.

But Ivana just shrugged. "Oh right, your sister is, like, in Rylan's crowd, right?" she said. "That's cool. So what's the real deal with this party?"

"No clue," Holly admitted. "Even Jennifer doesn't know where the party's going to be yet. It's, like, some huge secret. But don't worry. When I find out anything, you guys will be the first to know."

Emma tuned out again. Jackson was still there, just inches away. So close that she could reach out and run her fingers through his wavy brown hair. *If* she was the type of girl who did that sort of thing. Which she so totally wasn't.

She gulped as he leaned even closer. For one crazy second she imagined *he* wanted to run his hands through *her* hair and wished desperately that she'd left it loose and flowing around her shoulders instead of pulled back in its usual ponytail. Then she came back to her senses—sort of, anyway—and realized he didn't care about her hair. He was looking into her open locker.

"Cool door," he said.

"Oh, thanks?" Emma glanced at the interior of her locker door as if seeing it for the first time. It was like a miniature version of the inspiration wall in her studio. The only permanent part was a photo of her fashion idol, Coco Chanel. All around Coco floated a constantly changing mishmash of photos, clippings, scraps, and sketches held in place by magnets Emma had covered in a rainbow of cool fabrics.

Jackson pointed to a photo Emma had printed out in black and white. "I like that," he said.

"Thanks." She wasn't sure where this conversation was going. Or if they were even having a conversation. Not that it mattered. It was just weird to have him actually notice something of hers.

"It took me a second to figure out what it is. It's that archway leading between the middle-school and high-school halves of the building, right?" Jackson asked. "It looks totally different in close-up. Pretty cool."

Emma glanced at the photo with a jolt. He was right. That was exactly why she'd snapped the photo—to capture the small details and show them in a whole new way.

Emma looked at the photo again. She found herself flashing back to that old pink dress of Holly's. That was something else she thought needed a different focus, a new angle that would make people stop and look. Should that be how she approached the rest of her new holiday collection, too? She would have to think about it more, figure out how to make it work, but she was fairly sure Jackson's comment might have just sparked something great.

"Yeah, that's why I like the photo, too," she said. She almost forgot to be nervous and smiled at him.

He tilted his head away and kind of slid his eyes back toward her. It was hard to tell if he was smiling or what, but he looked happy.

Emma's skin tingled, and she tried desperately not to stare at him. For a second, it felt as if the two of them were alone in the hall.

But only for a second.

"Jackson," Lexie said. "Let's go. I need to get something out of my locker before homeroom." Lexie shot Emma a suspicious look as she led Jackson down the hall. Emma turned to watch him go, but Jackson never looked back.

CHAPTER 3

IN DEMAND

Y ou got here just in time, honey! I was about to pass out from severe lack of caffeine. I was *almost* desperate enough to attempt to choke down that toxic black sludge your father calls coffee."

Emma grinned as she and Charlie stepped out of the wheezy, old elevator. She needed a second to let her brain transition from the street-level cacophony of the Garment District to the cavernous, echoing, dusty halls of Laceland, her father's wholesale lace business. "No need. We're here to rescue you," she said.

Her father's long-time receptionist, Marjorie Kornbluth, stood behind the Formica-covered desk. She quickly checked her frosted lipstick, platinum-blond bob, and fake lashes in a tiny mirror, though Emma didn't know why she bothered. None of those things could move or had changed a bit, as far as Emma could tell, since way before she was born.

"I won't be long," Marjorie promised in her scratchy voice, snapping her mirror shut and tucking it into her black-leather satchel handbag. "I know you have a lot to do, *Allegra*."

Emma's grin widened. It was a relief to be here at Laceland, where everyone knew the truth.

"Oh, hey, yeah," she said. "When you get back, can you maybe give me a mini-lesson on how to deal with smocking? I have an idea to remake this kids' dress Holly gave me, but I want to figure out how to put it back together before I take it apart."

"Anything, honey. But trust me, you don't want me teaching you until I get some decent coffee in me." Marjorie winked.

One of the most surprising parts of Emma's Allegra adventures so far had been discovering that Marjorie wasn't just the most efficient receptionist this side of Broadway. She was also a skilled seamstress. She'd been a lifesaver when Emma was rushing to finish her first pieces for Paige. She owed Marjorie a lot. Not to mention her father, who paid her to help out around here, which in turn paid for most of her materials.

Charlie plopped into Marjorie's chair.

"I've got the phones," he said. "You go do the creative-genius thing."

"Really? You never do anything useful while you're here," Emma said.

"*So* not true," Charlie told her, feigning hurt. "I'm totally useful as an endless source of entertainment and moral support."

Emma laughed. "If *that's* what you call sitting around reading weirdo manga comics and listening to your iPod, then sure. You're way useful."

"*You're* going to answer phones?" Marjorie asked, looking Charlie up and down. "Color me skeptical."

"No, seriously. I can totally do this." Charlie cleared his throat, then grabbed the phone and spoke into it in a crisp British accent. "Good afternoon, Laceland. How may I be of service? Shipping and receiving? Please hold, madam."

Emma laughed. "Bravo! You must've inherited some of your mom's acting genes after all."

Marjorie pursed her lips. "I suppose it'll do. But no funny business, all right?"

"Nevah!" Charlie exclaimed in an even more pronounced accent, crossing his heart with one finger. "Your job is safe with me."

Marjorie chuckled as the elevator arrived. She disappeared into it, leaving behind a trail of her signature scent: eau de coffee and hairspray.

Emma shrugged and headed down the narrow hallway leading into the heart of the warehouse. She found her father in his office leaning over a bunch of lace samples with his warehouse manager, Isaac Muñoz. "Hi," she greeted them. "Need some help with that?"

"Hi there, Cookie," Noah Rose replied. "I think we're good. You might as well just head straight to your studio."

"Really?" Emma hesitated, feeling vaguely guilty. "I don't mind…"

"Go, go, save yourself!" Isaac told her and wriggled his slender fingers dramatically to shoo her off. "Do you think your father would offer if he didn't mean it? Please!" He slapped one hand to his carefully gelled hair in mock horror.

Emma giggled. Her father and Isaac were quite the odd couple. Noah Rose looked more like a linebacker than a guy who sold delicate, frilly lace for a living. He was easily twice the size of Isaac, though Isaac was at least twice as tightly wound as his boss and never stood still for more than half a second.

Emma scurried off to her sanctuary, her studio. That was a grand name for the small space tucked into the back corner of the warehouse behind a wall of filing cabinets. But that didn't matter. What mattered was that it was all hers.

Holly's old, pink smocked dress was draped over one of the stools in front of the huge metal worktable with its colorful collection of vintage cookie tins crammed full of ribbons, buttons, and all kinds of other treasures. Emma took the thick, plush, but slightly scratchy fabric between two fingers, rubbing it thoughtfully as ideas flitted through her head. She searched her inspiration wall until she found a photo.

She'd found it in a box at the very back of her closet shelf. The snapshot was taken on that warm winter day in the park. She and Holly grinned at the camera, their happy seven-year-old faces smeared with a rainbow of candy colors from the half-eaten lollipops they were clutching. Emma was wearing a kimono hoodie and fitted cords, and of course, Holly wore the pink smocked dress. The two friends looked so joyful and carefree that the photo made Emma smile every time she saw it. But it also made her sad. Would her friendship with Holly ever be the same again?

Eager to get started, she tacked the pink dress onto the front of one of the three dress forms she'd scavenged on 37th Street. Then she grabbed a fresh notebook and a handful of her Faber-Castell colored pencils; sat in front of her most beloved possession, the old but reliable Singer sewing machine that had been a

birthday gift from her Grandma Grace; and started sketching.

Isaac bustled past a little while later, pausing to peer into her studio. "I thought you were making grown-up clothes, not kiddie stuff," he said, breaking her out of her creative fog.

"I am." Emma stood and circled around Holly's dress, analyzing it from every angle. "This is the inspiration for my next collection. I'm working with the idea of little girls playing dress-up."

The idea had formed during science class that day. As Mr. Singh droned on about something environmental and boring, Emma had carefully pulled her sketchbook onto her lap to keep herself awake. She'd sketched out different ideas for reworking the pink dress, thinking about the way Holly had wanted to wear it everywhere and how much fun it had been to play dress-up at her apartment on Saturday. Then Emma had thought about Jackson's comment on that photo in her locker. About showing something old and ordinary in a new way. That was kind of her thing, anyway.

"I'm using typical little-girl clothes to add an unexpected twist to what are otherwise sleek and chic grown-up pieces," she explained to Isaac.

"Fab." Isaac nodded. "And so appropriate somehow for a fourteen-year-old designer, no?"

"Yep." She grinned at him. "I thought of that, too."

Charlie wandered in at that moment. "You thought of what?" he asked, as he tossed his backpack in a corner.

"It was all kind of inspired by Holly," Emma explained. She cast a critical eye on the pink frock. Yeah, she would definitely need Marjorie's help if she wanted to recreate the smocking. "See that photo?"

She pointed, and Charlie wandered closer. "Is that you and Holly?"

"Uh-huh. We were seven." Emma grabbed a swatch of charcoal-gray wool bouclé and held it up, debating whether it was sophisticated enough to counterbalance the sickly sweet pink. She pulled some plaid flannel scraps out of a bin under her desk and tried pinning those to the dress form as well.

Then she glanced over at the photo again. Despite her excitement about her new direction, Emma couldn't help sighing.

"What?" Charlie demanded.

"It still feels weird. Keeping such a huge secret from Holly, I mean. Especially now that the two of us are sort of back on track, friendship-wise."

Charlie flopped onto a wooden stool. "Seriously? Does that mean she's finally realized that Ivana Abbott is a waste of space?"

"Sadly, no." Emma made a wry face. "But she's been really cool about…" She stopped herself, realizing she'd been about to mention her crush on Jackson. Charlie didn't know about that. Even though she usually told him everything, she'd never quite gotten around to mentioning it.

Probably because she knew Charlie would mock him. Make fun of Jackson for hanging out with the shallow soccer boys. And she just didn't want to hear it. Not now. "Um, I mean, she was really cool when Rylan Sinclare was acting like a jerk the other day."

"Rylan Sinclare?" Charlie glanced up from fiddling with his iPod. "You mean that high-school snob who thinks she rules the school? Man, that girl's a freak. I heard she makes all her friends text her every morning to tell her what they're wearing. They're, like, never supposed to wear the same color as her, or something. Where'd you have the misfortune of running into her?"

"Holly's. Rylan is friends with Jen, remember?"

"Oh, right." He shrugged. "Sorry, guess I haven't been keeping track of the high-school social register. Whatever."

"Anyway," Emma said, "if I can make this big-girl, little-girl idea work, I think it will be really cool. Especially for the holiday season when everyone likes to dress up."

Charlie reached for Emma's sketchbook. He flipped through pages of rompers, baby-doll dresses, empire-waist dresses with edgy sashes, soft ruffles, and textured tights in high, strappy heels.

"Are all these new designs?" he asked. "They look good. Very Allegra. But I thought you only needed like six pieces for the pop-up shop."

"I do. But I keep having more ideas."

"You need to narrow them down soon if you're going to finish in time."

Emma raised an eyebrow. "Oh, come on. You're suddenly turning into the voice of responsibility?"

Charlie grinned. "What can I say? I like to keep you on your toes."

A phone buzzed, and Emma dug through a pile of fabric on her worktable. "The Allegra phone. I think I set it down here somewhere."

"Got it." Charlie pushed aside a stack of zippers and grabbed the cherry-red phone. Without bothering to check who was calling, he flipped it open and pressed it to his ear. "Allegra Biscotti International," he said in his crisp British-secretary voice. "How may I direct your call?" He listened for a second and then spoke again in his normal voice. "Yeah, she's right here." Tossing the phone to Emma, he said, "Paige."

"Paige? Hi," Emma said into the phone, suddenly nervous. What if the editor was calling to tell her that the powers-that-be at *Madison* had decided not to include Allegra Biscotti in the pop-up after all?

"Emma. How's the new collection going?" Paige called out.

"Fine so far," Emma said. "I—"

"Great, great, fantastic." Paige sounded even more frazzled than usual. "Listen, something else just came up."

"Something else?" Emma echoed cautiously.

"One of the vice presidents of *Madison*'s parent company was just here. Some corporate suit from up on the top floor. I have no idea what he does, but his signature is on all my paychecks. His daughter saw your designs on the magazine's blog, and now she wants Allegra Biscotti to design a fabulous one-of-a-kind dress for some insanely opulent party she's throwing.

"It's going to be at that super-luxe new members-only club in Chelsea that everyone's talking about—Chateau. You know it? Anyway, Daddy Dearest must've laid out a fortune and a half to book *that* place, and he's ready to pay big bucks for this dress, too."

"Um, okay?" Emma always had trouble keeping up when Paige started talking a million miles a minute. "When's the party?"

"That's the crazy part. It's late next month—actually, the same weekend as the pop-up shop."

"What?" Emma shook her head even though she knew Paige couldn't see her. It was going to be hard enough to finish six pieces in time for the grand opening. No way could she design an extra dress on top of that! At least not without dropping out of school and giving up sleep. And she had a feeling her parents weren't going to go for either of those options.

"I already said yes," Paige informed her. "I didn't have a choice, if you know what I mean." She sighed loudly. "Oh, and I almost forgot. The party girl goes to your school. Her name is Rylan Sinclare."

CHAPTER 4

WRINKLES

R-Rylan Sinclare?" Emma stammered, wondering if they had a bad phone connection. No, *hoping* they had a bad connection.

"Do you know her?" Paige asked.

"Yes. No. Sort of. Not exactly," Emma stumbled.

"Hmm. Well, figure it out, because we're meeting with Rylan and her mother on Friday afternoon."

"A meeting?" If Emma had felt overwhelmed by the thought of layering another project on top of her other work, like adding a wool vest on top of a puffy down jacket, she was absolutely stunned now. Design a dress for Rylan Sinclare? *The* Rylan Sinclare? The girl would tear her apart—without the aid of a seam ripper.

"Yes, of course." Paige was beginning to sound impatient. "How else are you going to make a custom dress for her?"

Emma clutched her phone tighter, ignoring Charlie's curious stare as he listened to her side of the conversation. "Um, okay, yeah, I get that," she said. "But how am I supposed to pull this off? I mean, aren't they going to be surprised when I show up to meet her? Especially if she recognizes me from school?"

Fat chance that will ever happen. Rylan probably didn't know she existed. Well, not unless she happened to remember the weird girl in the weirder outfit she'd made fun of at Jennifer's apartment the other day.

"Don't worry about that," Paige said. "I'm already working on a plan. But I'll have to fill you in later, okay? I'm way late for my next meeting. *Ciao!*" The line cut off.

"What was that all about?" Charlie asked as Emma hung up and dropped the phone back onto the worktable.

"Allegra just got commissioned to design a party dress for a rich private client," she whispered, still trying to make sense of it all.

His eyes went wide. "Rylan Sinclare? For real? *She's* your first client?"

Emma nodded and then quickly filled him in on the details—or at least as many as Paige had shared with her. By the end, Charlie was shaking his head.

"What a waste," he declared, kicking at the leg of the

battered stool he was sitting on. "Allegra's designs are too good for Rylan and the rest of the superficial squad at Downtown Day."

"I don't know," Emma mumbled, still too shocked to really take this all in. "Rylan's a snob, but she does know how to dress."

Charlie didn't seem to hear her. "I know!" he exclaimed, jumping to his feet and pacing restlessly across the room, dodging dress forms. "This could be your chance to get back at her for all the stuck-up crap she's ever done. I mean, she's a total label Mabel, right?"

"A what?"

"Yeah, I just made that up." Charlie stopped and smiled, looking pleased with himself. "A label Mabel is, like, a person who cares more about the label than anything else. Like, she'd wear a plastic tablecloth if some foo-foo designer slapped their label on it. You know the type."

Ivana and her followers flashed in Emma's mind. They fit the definition.

"So all you have to do is have Allegra design the ugliest dress in the world." Charlie waved his hands around, looking more excited by the second. "Like, I'm talking full-out repulsive, maybe gold lamé with pink fur trim and a matching sombrero. As long as it's got the Allegra Biscotti label on it, she'll wear it!" Then he gasped. "Ooh! Or even better—you could totally go all Emperor's New Clothes on her! Just think of the reaction when she walks into her own party wearing nothing but her unmentionables."

Emma couldn't help laughing at his enthusiasm. She relaxed, at least a little. "Okay, picturing that just might help me survive," she said. "But I hate to break it to you—it's not going to happen for real. Allegra's rep is at stake. Besides, I'd never do that to someone, not even Rylan Sinclare."

"Yeah, you've always been too nice," Charlie said. "It's one of your worst qualities."

She grinned. "Thanks, pal."

"You're welcome, pal. So you're going to design Rylan some fabulous Allegra dress?"

"I don't have a choice," Emma said. "Anyway, it shouldn't be *too* hard to fit it in. I mean it's not like I have to design and sew a whole collection in a few weeks. Hey, what's one more dress?"

She took a deep breath. Allegra's life definitely moved at a much faster pace than Emma's.

"I guess she's going to have to like one of the designs I'll work up for the pop-up shop. Once I've figured out the design, maybe Marjorie can help me out with the sewing." She bit her lip. "I just hope Paige's plan is epic, because otherwise I'm really not seeing how I'm going to pull off this meeting."

"I can *do* this," Emma whispered, staring at the framed Coco Chanel picture in her locker. "I *can* do this. *I* can do this."

"Em, there you are!" Holly's voice sang out.

Emma spun around and watched Holly expertly dodge and weave through the pre-homeroom throngs in the school hallway. Ivana was by her side. Both looked majorly excited, though Emma didn't have the mental energy to wonder why. It was Tuesday morning, and she'd spent the entire subway ride to school trying to figure out how she was going to fit Rylan's dress design into her already packed schedule for the next few weeks. Assuming that Paige came up with some miracle solution to the meeting dilemma, that is, which still didn't seem like a sure thing to Emma.

Holly and Ivana slid to a stop in front of her. "Huge news!" Holly squealed, grabbing Emma by the arm. "We just found out where Rylan's Sweet Sixteen is going to be!"

"Yeah, me too," Emma said, still distracted by her own thoughts. She visualized her sketches—the babydoll mini, Holly's velvet smock-dress, a tiered princess-gown concept she was playing around with, and a super-simple, sashed party dress...Would one of these be right for Rylan? "It's at some fancy new club called Chateau."

There was a moment of silence. That finally broke Emma

out of her mental sketchbook. She blinked, realizing that Holly and Ivana were both staring at her, shocked.

"Um, how'd you hear?" Holly asked.

Her voice sounded fairly normal. But her expression spoke louder than her words. Emma felt uncomfortable as she realized that this was where their friendship was now. Holly was "the cool one," the one who was supposed to find out about important news like major high-school parties. Emma was the one who would be forever hopelessly clueless, verging on nerdy.

"Uh…" Emma thought fast. "Charlie told me?"

Holly seemed willing to accept that. But Ivana narrowed her eyes. "You mean weirdo Charlie Calhoun you're always hanging around with?" she said. "How would *he* find out something like that?"

"I don't know." Emma busied herself rearranging books in her locker to avoid their stares. "I guess he overheard some high-school kids talking about it."

"Come on, Ivana." Holly blew a bright citrusy-orange bubble and popped it. "Let's go find Lexie. She'll die when she hears this! She's been talking about Chateau ever since her mom covered the big grand opening last month on the eleven o'clock news."

"Okay," Ivana said.

Emma didn't pull her head out of her locker until she was sure they were gone. Even then, she could still feel Ivana's eyes boring into her.

"So you're sure you won't reconsider my ugly-dress plan?" Charlie asked. "I could help you go Dumpster diving for some awesome materials."

Emma laughed as she entered the lobby of her building. Charlie had just called. He had a paper due the next day, so he'd gone straight home from school instead of meeting at Laceland.

"What's that music in the background?" Emma asked.

Charlie groaned. "Don't ask. Mom's teaching a class called Musical Theater for Beginners. She should have called it Musical Theater for the Tone Deaf."

Emma winced as she heard someone start belting out an enthusiastic but off-key version of "Hello, Dolly." There was a reason they didn't hang out at Charlie's apartment much.

"Anyway," she said, "I'm going to bring all of the sketches of the dresses I'm thinking about for the pop-up shop tomorrow. I thought that would be a good place to start to see what Rylan likes."

Charlie had already agreed to come along for moral

support. And Paige had agreed that Charlie could come only after Emma explained to her how unbearably nervous she was about meeting with Rylan. Here was the plan: Emma and Charlie would both be posing as Allegra's interns, as they'd done before. They had fooled Paige with that routine, for a little while anyhow.

Emma felt her heart clench. Paige still hadn't filled her in on the rest of her plan yet. If Emma was going to be an intern, who was going to be Allegra? She stepped into the elevator and pressed the button for the eighteenth floor, trying not to panic. Paige hadn't let her down so far, had she? Emma just had to trust her. What choice did she have?

"Maybe Rylan will just pick one of the designs," she told Charlie. "I sketched out a bunch of different options."

"Oh." She could almost hear Charlie's shrug over the phone, even over the cringe-inducing background singing. He was totally invested in Allegra, but he was never too interested in the actual details of the sewing part. "Okay. So back to the pop-up stuff. When are you hitting Allure?"

"Soon. Maybe Saturday."

Emma felt a shiver of excitement. She loved Allure Fabrics, with its floor-to-ceiling racks of textiles of every description. She could—and sometimes did—spend all day wandering the cramped aisles, drinking in the sight and touch and smell of the silks and the poplins, the eyelets and brocades, the crisp cottons and flowing chiffons. Thousands of bolts of fabric in every weight, every texture, every shade of the rainbow. Dreaming of all the clothes yet to be imagined, designed, and created.

"The best part is," she added, switching the phone to her other ear, "I won't be working on a super-tight budget for once. I still can't believe how much Rylan's parents are willing to shell out for this one dress. I almost died when Paige told me."

"A true silver lining," Charlie agreed.

"Lining, get it? See what I did there? Sewing humor."

Emma dug out her keys as she reached her front door. "If you say *sew*," she replied. "Ha-ha. I can do it, too. Anyway, I'll be able to afford really top-of-the-line material…"

Her voice trailed off as she entered the apartment and heard her mother call out her name. A second later Joan Rose appeared around the corner, looking excited.

"Emma!" she exclaimed. "Big news!"

"Got to go," Emma told Charlie. "Call you later." Clicking off her phone, she dropped her bag on the worn gingham fabric of the front-hall bench. "What's up?" she asked.

Her mother smiled and tugged on a strand of gray-tinged

brown hair that had come loose from her sloppy bun. She had one of Noah's oversized wool sweaters wrapped around her, which probably meant the heat was on the fritz again. The mass of mud-brown wool might be cozy, but it didn't do much for her look.

Joan Rose lived in an interchangeable, bland sea of sensible slacks, comfortable shoes, and organic cotton tops that Emma had long ago dubbed Academic Drab. And no matter what Emma did, she couldn't convince her mother to brighten up her so-called style. She couldn't even talk her into updating the green plastic glasses she'd been wearing for as long as Emma could remember.

"I just found out you made the cut," Joan said, shoving the glasses farther up her nose. "You're going to be in Betsy's western civ class next semester!"

"Oh." Emma shrugged off her brown velvet trench coat as she took in the news. She'd almost forgotten about that. Her mom had insisted she try out for a special class that her mother's best friend, Betsy Ling, taught every second semester at Downtown Day. The test had been tough, and Emma had assumed she probably wouldn't get in. Not that she cared—she certainly wasn't begging for more homework. "Um, that's cool, I guess."

"Cool?" Her mother sighed. "Humor me here, Emma. This is big news. You won't believe how much you're going to learn from Betsy. It's going to open all kinds of doors for you." She clasped her hands together, beaming happily. "As soon as this fashion-shop business is out of the way, maybe you and I can spend the holiday season hitting some museums. You know, get you a little head start before the class starts up in January? What do you say?"

Emma didn't know what to say. She was stuck on the first part: "*As soon as this fashion-shop business is out of the way.*" Did she think that this was it for Allegra? That when the pop-up shop closed down, Emma would just go back to her ordinary life?

Then again, why was she even surprised? Her mom was pretty cool in a lot of ways. She tried really hard to stay out of Emma's face at Downtown Day, where she taught English over in the high school. But it was fairly clear that she'd never really understood Emma's passion for fashion. She seemed to think her daughter's obsession with clothes was something she'd eventually outgrow, like unicorn stickers and hating cooked carrots.

At least she's letting me do the pop-up shop collection, Emma reminded herself. After the way Emma had kept Allegra a secret from them in the beginning, she knew her parents could have put an end to the whole thing. Instead they'd allowed her to move ahead with it and were even fronting the money for materials.

Okay, so Emma's dad was probably the more enthusiastic one—after all, he was in the fashion business himself, at least in a peripheral way. Her mom, on the other hand, seemed to be treating the whole situation as some huge extra-credit project, something that would be forgotten as soon as the grades were in.

Still, Emma figured the least she could do was pretend to be happy about this extra class for her mom's sake. After all, school was her mom's life. Emma got that. She just wished that once in a while her mom could at least pretend to understand that fashion was *Emma's* life—and that that would never, ever change.

"Out," Emma ordered as she stepped into her room after dinner and spotted her ten-year-old brother, William, crouching in front of her bookshelf.

William scowled at her. "Chillax, spaz girl. I was just checking to see if you have any books about ancient Greece. I have a stupid report due tomorrow."

"My room isn't the public library."

William made a mean face at her and stalked out. Emma shut the door behind him and flopped onto her bed, which was adorned with dozens of pillows she had sewn with her fabric scraps, working them into increasingly complicated patterns. When Grandma Grace had first given her the sewing machine, she'd had Emma practice by sewing fabric scraps together. These grew into quilt-like swaths of material that were then stuffed and sewn up to make pillows. Emma still found it relaxing and rewarding to turn her scraps into colorful accessories.

She reached for the basket where she kept the glossy, exotic foreign fashion magazines she bought at her favorite magazine shop near Bryant Park. Right now she had everything from the French and Italian editions of *Madison* and the British *Tatler* to more obscure choices like *Baila* and *Egg* from Japan and *Unfair* from Abu Dhabi.

Dumping them all out, she flipped through pages, still focused on Rylan's dress. Could she really pull this off? Could she and Paige convince super-finicky Rylan that she was really working with some big-time international designer like the ones in these magazines?

She tossed aside the magazines and rolled onto her back. She found herself staring at a drawing hanging on the bulletin board by her desk. Not one of hers. Jackson's. He was into comic-book art, and he'd sketched a cool action shot of a character that looked like an ordinary kid crossed with a superhero. When Emma had admired it, he'd ripped it out of his notebook and given it to her.

Now it was hanging where she could see it from every

part of the room. At first, looking at it made her shiver. But now that Jackson and Lexie seemed to be so tight, it just gave her one more reason to wonder why everything in life had to be so complicated. She should be excited about the pop-up shop deal, but now she had this extra thing with Rylan to stress about. Just like she should be thrilled that Jackson had given her his sketch, except what was the point when he was with Lexie?

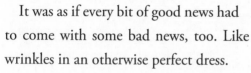

It was as if every bit of good news had to come with some bad news, too. Like wrinkles in an otherwise perfect dress.

Her cell phone rang, pulling her out of her thoughts.

"I just heard the cool news!" Holly exclaimed. "I wanted to call and congratulate you."

Emma's head spun. The cool news? Was she talking about the pop-up shop? About Allegra? Had Holly found out her secret?

"Um, what?" she blurted out.

"The Western Civ class," Holly prompted. "Lexie got in, too. She said she saw your name on the list. Didn't you hear yet?"

"Oh, yeah." Emma's heartbeat slowed to normal. Holly

hadn't discovered the truth about Allegra Biscotti. Just about the stupid extra class. She couldn't drag enough pep into her voice to fake that she cared. "Mom just told me, actually."

"Oh. Aren't you excited? You sound kind of weird."

Emma hesitated, wishing she could tell Holly about the whole Rylan situation. As strange as it seemed, Holly was now the best person Emma knew at dealing with popular kids. And popular high-school kids—well, forget that.

But she couldn't tell her. Not without giving everything away. "No, it's cool," she said. "I'm just in a funk about trying to finish all those geometry problems we got for homework tonight."

Holly laughed and said something, but Emma hardly heard her. She was thinking that this was just another wrinkle— having something completely amazing like Allegra Biscotti happen, but not being able to share it with her best friend.

CHAPTER 5

BELLISSIMA

Emma leaned her elbows on the cafeteria table and stared at Holly, mentally redressing her in the new version of Holly's pink velvet dress she'd been working on. Emma had decided on a brown plaid flannel to contrast with the girliness of the princess pink. She would add panels of the flannel on the sides to expand the bodice to a grown-up size, and the flannel would be used to extend the puffy, pink cap sleeves so they would end at the elbow in soft, brown plaid. Emma still needed to search for just the right buttons for the French cuffs she'd designed. This contrast of girly and serious, young and sophisticated, was going to set the tone for all of her pieces.

As Holly laughed and moved around in her seat, reacting to whatever stupid stuff Ivana and the others were saying, Emma desperately hoped she'd have the chance to give the dress to Holly and to come clean about the whole Allegra thing…

"Earth to Emma!"

Emma blinked, realizing that Holly was waving a hand in front of her face. "Um, what?" Emma said. "Sorry, I was thinking about something."

"Obviously." Holly smiled. "I said, are you going to eat the rest of your chips? Shaye's been staring at them like a hungry hyena."

"Help yourself." Emma pushed the half-eaten bag of chips across the table toward Shannon.

"Thanks." Shannon grabbed the bag and stuffed a few chips into her mouth. Even Emma, who tried not to pay any more attention to the Bees than she had to, had noticed that Shannon always seemed to be ravenous these days. Probably because she'd been growing so fast that she was almost as tall as Holly, though so far the growth spurt hadn't added any curves to Shannon's athletic body.

"Gross. I don't know how anyone eats that garbage." Ivana wrinkled her nose, sipped delicately at her flavored water, and then glanced around the table. "Is someone's phone turned on?" she added. "I hear buzzing."

"Not me," Kayla said. "Mr. Manning threatened to have me expelled if he caught me texting in the caf one more time."

When the phone buzzed again, Emma realized it was coming from the pocket of her heather-gray cardigan. Oops. She had left her regular phone in her locker. There were strict school rules about that. But she'd forgotten that the

Allegra phone was tucked in the pocket of her sweater when she had grabbed it from her locker before lunch.

"I think it's me," she said, reaching into the oversized pocket. She glanced down, raising the phone slightly to get a look at the caller ID without letting anyone else see. *Paige Young*, the readout blinked.

Holly leaned across the table and caught a glimpse of the cherry-colored flip. "Hey, that's not your regular phone!" she exclaimed. "Sweet! Why didn't you tell me you got a new one?"

She lunged across the table, making a move to grab it. Panicking, Emma jerked back to keep it out of her reach. What if Holly recognized Paige's name on the readout? She and the other girls read *Madison* almost as religiously as Emma did. She had to grab the edge of the table to keep from ending up splayed on the floor.

"Hey!" Ivana complained as the table shook, almost tipping over her cherry nonfat yogurt. "Do you mind? Some of us are trying to eat here."

"Sorry," Emma mumbled, feeling stupid as she pushed the phone down into her pocket. "Um, Holly startled me."

"Oh. Sorry." Holly looked confused.

Ivana's eyes darted from Emma's face to her sweater, as

if calculating whether what had just happened was worth commenting on. Deciding not to give her the chance, Emma stood. "I just remembered I, uh, have a book I'm supposed to get back to the library before the end of today," she said. "Better go take care of that. Bye."

She hurried away with Holly's "Later, Em!" floating after her. None of the others said anything. They'd probably already forgotten she was ever there. Not that Emma cared. She only sat with them because Holly pretty much insisted, waving and yoo-hooing the second Emma entered the cafeteria every day.

So far Emma hadn't had the heart to ignore her and sit down somewhere else, but it was starting to get tempting. True, Charlie claimed to be allergic to the cafeteria and ate in the student lounge most of the time. But he wasn't her only other friend at Downtown Day. She could easily find another group to sit with. A group that wouldn't act as if they were doing her a favor by allowing her brown-bag lunch to rest on the same table as theirs.

Safely tucked away in the far stall in the girls' bathroom, Emma pulled out the Allegra phone. A text from Paige reminded her about the meeting that afternoon and ordered her to arrive a little early, so they could get their stories straight. The text ended with a cryptic message:

My plan will kill 3 huge birds w 1 glam stone!

Emma had no idea what that meant.

"Chill out, would you?" Charlie complained. "I'm getting seasick." He clamped a hand on Emma's knee, which was bouncing around as she tapped her foot anxiously.

"I can't help it. I'm crazy nervous." Emma pushed away his hand and kept tapping. "I still don't see how Paige thinks we're going to pull this off."

Charlie lounged back in the hard, plastic subway seat, his long legs stretching out almost to the black platform boots of the girl dressed all in black sitting across from them reading *People* magazine. "Maybe she's going to hypnotize Rylan and her mom," he joked. "You'll be standing there in front of them, but they'll see some glamorous Italian fashionista."

"Yeah, that could work." Emma rolled her eyes.

The subway screeched to a halt at Times Square. Emma gave Charlie a sharp poke in the shoulder. "We're here."

Soon they were climbing the steps, leaving the dankness of the subway station for the crisp winter air of the mid-Manhattan streets. Emma always found it fascinating how different the crowds could be in different parts of the city. Back in SoHo, where they'd started, the pedestrians varied

cape

cape 2.0

from local artists dressed in funky individual styles to tourists window-shopping at the galleries and boutiques.

Now, as she and Charlie emerged from the subway, they were surrounded by tourists, office workers, theater types, and panhandlers. Once they headed east into the heart of Midtown's business district, they found themselves swimming through a sea of suits, from serious banker-wear to the more fashionable cuts and fabrics favored by those in publishing and entertainment.

But today she could hardly focus on any of that. "I can't believe we're actually going to *Madison*'s offices," she said, peering up at the sleek, black-glass high-rise building they were approaching.

Charlie shrugged. "What's the big? We've been here before."

"Yeah, but we never got past the lobby." The two of them had dropped off a dress for Paige in the days before the editor knew Allegra Biscotti's true identity. "This time we're going upstairs—to the actual offices where they create the bible of the fashion universe!"

"Dramatic much?" Charlie grinned. "I'm sure it's just some rooms full of Xerox machines and stale coffee, like every other office in the world."

But Emma wasn't convinced. She held her breath for most of the way up to the seventeenth floor. Luckily the elevator was fast, and moments later they were stepping off the elevator.

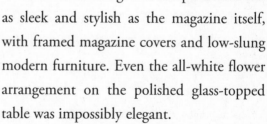

Emma sucked in her breath again as she looked around the airy, gardenia-scented lobby. She was glad to have Charlie there to lead the way over to the reception desk because she wasn't sure she'd ever have found the nerve to approach the stunningly gorgeous young woman sitting there. The receptionist wore a simple cocoa shift dress, and the colorful silk scarf knotted at her neck was the perfect finishing touch.

But Charlie was intimidated by no one. He marched right over, announcing that they were there to see Paige and leaving Emma free to look around, not even wanting

to waste time blinking. The reception area was as sleek and stylish as the magazine itself, with framed magazine covers and low-slung modern furniture. Even the all-white flower arrangement on the polished glass-topped table was impossibly elegant.

Then a young woman in her twenties with a high, sleek ponytail appeared. Emma wondered how she could walk, much less walk *quickly* in her four-inch-high ankle boots.

"Oh, hi," she said, making a beeline for Emma and Charlie. "I've seen you before. Allegra Biscotti's interns, right?"

"That's us," Charlie said.

Emma just nodded. She'd seen Ponytail Girl before, too. She was Paige's assistant. Emma knew she should say hi. But she couldn't speak. She couldn't even believe she was really here. Even after all the crazy, amazing stuff that had happened lately—meeting Paige at Laceland and having Allegra's designs featured on the magazine's website—this was the gold button on the Chanel suit. She was walking into *Madison*'s offices for a meeting with the senior fashion editor and her first client! Unreal.

Her eyes darted around, still trying to take in as much as possible as Ponytail Girl led them down a plush-carpeted hallway lined with more framed *Madison* covers. Fabulously fashionable people looking busy and important glided in and out of offices that were like little jewel boxes. Emma was so distracted by super-high heels covered in hot pink snakeskin and deep purple suede that she almost lost Paige's assistant in a row of cubicles.

Emma peered into one doorway and knew instantly what was inside: the infamous fashion closet. She was pretty sure there had to be an accessories closet somewhere nearby,

but she didn't have time to look for it. They'd reached Paige's office.

"There you are!" Paige glanced up as they entered and then pushed aside the papers she'd been looking at so abruptly that she almost knocked over the paper cup of takeout coffee on the glass-topped mahogany desk. "Get in here. We need to talk." Noticing Ponytail Girl still hovering eagerly in the doorway, Paige frowned. "Did you suddenly forget how to walk, Caroline?" she snapped. "Out!"

Caroline scurried away, pulling the door shut behind her. Emma glanced around at Paige's office. It was as tastefully appointed as Paige herself. Tone-on-tone taupe upholstery on the guest chairs, fresh flowers in muted pinks and whites arranged in cut-crystal vases on the small end tables, framed black-and-white photos on the walls.

But she barely had time to take it all in—Paige was already talking.

"This is the plan, okay?" she was saying briskly. "You two are the interns. *Just* the interns. When the Sinclares get here, we pretend we're waiting for Allegra. She's due to arrive any second from, I don't know, a photo shoot out in Brooklyn Heights or something. We make small talk, whatever. After a minute or two, my phone rings—it's Allegra. She's calling from the airport to apologize. She just found out she has to jet off to Europe on some fashion emergency."

"Fashion emergency?" Charlie put in. "Like what? Someone wore white after Labor Day?"

"White works year round," Paige told him. "Anyway, I don't know. Problems with a supplier or maybe some kind of fashion-show thing…" She gave him a slightly irritated look. "I'll come up with something. Anyway, she'll authorize her talented staff to stand in for her at this meeting, take notes and get the girl's measurements and email it all to her over in Europe—"

"Wait." Emma had been with her up until now. In fact, she was impressed. Paige's plan was so simple it seemed obvious now. But it seemed even the best plans had a fatal wrinkle. "Measurements?" she said, shaking her head. "Sorry, but I really can't see myself taking Rylan's measurements. I doubt she's going to go for me touching her either."

"I'll do it," Charlie volunteered.

Paige rolled her eyes. "Yeah, not," she told him. Then she glanced at Emma. "Don't freak out. I have a plan for that part, too." Striding over to her desk, she leaned over and punched a button on the phone. "Caroline!" she called into the intercom. "Send Francesca in."

There was hardly time to wonder who Francesca was when the door opened, admitting the tallest, most exotically gorgeous young woman Emma had ever seen outside the pages of *Madison* itself. She was in her early twenties, with long, gloriously wavy chestnut-colored hair that tumbled over slim shoulders encased in a luscious, caramel-colored, merino-wool ribbed turtleneck.

"*Ciao!*" the young woman said, flashing a huge, brilliant smile.

"Come on in, Francesca." Paige hurried over and closed the door. "Meet Emma and Charlie."

"Oh, Emma!" Francesca exclaimed in a thick Italian accent. She rushed over and clasped Emma's hands tightly in her own. Close up, she smelled like Mediterranean sunshine and olive groves. Or at least what Emma imagined Mediterranean sunshine and olive groves must smell like. "I have been hearing so much about you, *cara mia!*"

"Francesca's from Italy," Paige said.

"You don't say?" Charlie smirked.

Paige ignored him, speaking to Emma. "Her father is an important advertising client. Cars or something."

"Timepieces, actually," Francesca put in with a giggle. She sank down onto one of the guest chairs and crossed her long legs, giving Emma a better view of her walnut-brown suede stilettos. "Papa, he is the watch king of Europe."

"Whatever." Paige waved her hand, her cushion-cut engagement ring glinting. "Anyway, Francesca's been interning at the magazine, trying to break into the fashion biz. But she screwed up one too many times, and the editor-in-chief wants her out of her *coiffure*."

Francesca giggled again. "I am afraid *Signorina* Paige is correct," she told Emma and Charlie with a charming little shrug. "*Signora* has little patience. Without Paige, I would already be on an airplane back to Napoli, I fear."

"And don't you forget it," Paige warned Francesca. "Remember, this little job is top secret. I don't know how to say that in Italian, but I'm really hoping we don't need a translator here."

"*Si, capisco*," Francesca said. "My lips, they are zipped!" She made a zipping gesture across her perfectly lined, cranberry-slicked lips.

Emma felt a jolt as she caught on to what they were saying. "Wait," she said carefully. "So Francesca knows…everything?"

"Well, she doesn't know much about typing. Or filing. Or anything like that." Paige shrugged. "But Allegra Biscotti? Yeah, she knows the whole deal. But don't worry. She'll keep your secret. She owes me that much."

Francesca nodded enthusiastically. "*Si, si!*" she exclaimed.

"It's a brilliant plan, if I do say so myself," Paige said. "We introduce Francesca today as Allegra's personal assistant and fashion apprentice. She can take the girl's measurements.

You said you had some fashion-school training back in Italy, right?" she added, pointing a flawlessly French-manicured finger at Francesca.

"*Si*, of course!" Francesca began. "I was—"

"Never mind, we don't need the details," Paige interrupted. She turned her attention back to Emma. "Plus, she'll be the perfect public face for Allegra Biscotti moving forward. We can use her for face-to-face stuff, like the opening-night press party for the pop-up shop. That accent will sound killer to your clients, too. We need to get her to record a new message for Allegra's voice mail pronto."

"It's good." Emma had to admit that Francesca was going to look and sound a lot more impressive than a couple of middle-schoolers. Rylan and her mother probably wouldn't even notice that she and Charlie were in the room once they got a load of her. Paige had come through for her yet again.

"This will be so exciting!" Francesca uncrossed her legs and perched on the edge of the chair, her dark eyes flashing with excitement. "And it is such an honor to be working with such a talented new designer as you, Emmita. If it is possible, would you please show me your designs for this dress?"

"Um, sure." Emma was glad that Francesca seemed completely unfazed by her young age. She reached into her messenger bag and pulled out the teal brocade sketchbook where she'd made the sketches for this meeting. Emma opened up to the first page of dress sketches and began to explain to Francesca and Paige, "For the pop-up store, I'm doing a bunch of dresses that *almost* look like they could be little girls' party dresses. But each one has a really sophisticated twist, so they're both young and old at the same time."

"Love, love, *love* the idea," interrupted Paige.

Emma couldn't believe that Paige was being supportive. She stood there speechless, grinning.

"Enough about the pop-up store. Show me what you've got for this Rylan," Paige ordered, immediately switching moods. "They're going to be buzzing any second."

"I was hoping Rylan would like one of the dresses I'm designing for the pop-up shop," Emma said, "because I don't think I can design and make seven pieces in four weeks." Paige looked at her with cold eyes. "I still have to go to school," Emma explained shyly.

This brought Paige back to earth. "Of course, you do. You're a child! Okay. Show me," she ordered.

Emma dutifully walked Paige through the designs. She'd decided not to show Rylan the piece she'd designed from Holly's smocked dress. First off, it was one of a kind, and second, it was more casual than Emma imagined Chateau would be. She showed Paige her other three dress ideas, any of which she could see on Rylan or any other chic young woman.

"First, there's the baby-doll minidress." Emma told them

she'd envisioned it in candy-colored silk—like a swirly
lollipop. She had yet to look at fabrics at Allure, but she was
sure she'd find something perfect.

Paige's eyebrows arched when Emma pulled
out the next sketch she'd done for the leggings.
"I want to try layering fishnet or lacy stocking
over sheer tights. The dress is so short it needs
something more than tights but not quite
leggings." Emma had loved the look when
she spotted it on those hip European tourists and wanted to try her own version. She
was going to ask her dad if he had any kind
of stretchy, loose-weave lace. Otherwise
she'd pick up some fishnets and go to
town with her scissors.

Paige was strangely quiet, which made Emma even more
nervous. Her only response was to flip to the next page, which
showed about four different versions of Emma's take on a
lacy tiered princess dress—if the princess lived in Manhattan.
It had a racy top, and Emma was playing with bold colors—
each tier or layer in a different shade—turquoise and lime or
burnt orange and deep magenta. Colors that were anything
but prim, quiet, and childish.

The last dress she showed them was the one she thought
Rylan would like best. It was so simple, yet she had struggled

to get it just right: a grown-up version of a little girl's party dress. The basic dress was, well, basic. She was thinking that a stretchy satin or even some kind of weave would work. It was all about the enormous sash—in a contrasting color and fabric—that could be tied so many different ways.

Emma had sketched a few different versions—with long sleeves or no sleeves, with a simple crew neck, or a wide boatneck, backless, or with a high back. And on the next few pages, she showed the many ideas she had for tying the oversized sash. Front and center in an elaborate bow. Crisscrossing in back, crisscrossing in front. Wrapping around the waist several times to make a wide sash with a tiny knot in the front or back, which was her favorite. Then she fanned out a bunch of fabric swatches she'd pulled from her big bin to show Rylan and her mom how she, well, Allegra, would contrast something stretchy and textured with something smooth and shiny.

Paige slid back behind her desk, folding her hands in front of her. "You're off to a good start, Emma. Let's just hope the Sinclares think so. They *are* the clients."

Emma breathed, relieved, as Francesca reached for the sketchbook. "Be careful, there are some—"

Francesca immediately fumbled and dropped the sketchbook, sending a shower of fabric swatches and a dozen or so buttons across Paige's spotless office.

Emma dropped to her knees, scrambling to grab whatever she could. Charlie did the same.

"Oops!" Francesca giggled apologetically. "I am...how do you say it? A butterfingers? Such an odd word, but *Signora* Editor-in-Chief uses it often."

Paige swore softly under her breath. "Never mind," she snapped, bending to grab a tiny beaded button just before it rolled under her desk. "Let's just get this mess picked up before—"

The buzz of the intercom interrupted. "Paige?" the pony-tailed assistant chirped. "The Sinclares are here."

CHAPTER 6

CLIENT RELATIONS

Emma wasn't sure how they did it. But in the two or three minutes between the assistant's call and the Sinclares' arrival, she, Charlie, Francesca, and Paige managed to get everything picked up and tucked safely away in the sketchbook.

Almost everything.

As the door started to open, Emma spied one last button lying next to Paige's desk. She dove to grab it but wasn't quick enough to get back on her feet again before Rylan swept into the office, followed by her mother.

Paige didn't miss a beat. Ignoring the fact that Emma was on her hands and knees staring up at the new arrivals with her mouth hanging open, the fashion editor stepped forward with her hand extended.

"Hello, Mrs. Sinclare. Rylan," she said. "I'm Paige Young. So wonderful to finally meet you. Thank you for coming."

"Good afternoon," Mrs. Sinclare said, shaking her hand. "Lovely to meet you as well."

Emma scrambled to her feet, her cheeks flaming. She forced a smile as Paige turned to nod toward her.

"This is Emma Rose, one of Allegra Biscotti's interns," Paige said. "She was just picking up something she dropped."

Emma felt like a mustard stain on a couture outfit as both Rylan and her mother glanced her way. "Um, hi," she mumbled.

Rylan stared at her. "Rose? Hang on, I think I know you," she said. "You're my English teacher's kid, right?"

"Right." Emma smiled weakly, not sure whether to be flattered or terrified that Rylan knew who she was.

Rylan lifted one perfectly plucked eyebrow in surprise. "Aren't you, like, in middle school? And you're a fashion intern? How'd you land that gig?"

Mrs. Sinclare shot a look at her diamond Chopard watch. "If you don't mind, we need to get this show on the road," she said. "I have a lot to do today."

Emma would have known the woman was Rylan's mother anywhere. She had the same air of authority, along with the same long nose and close-together eyes, though her hair was dyed ash blond and swept into a chic loose bun, and her fitted, black bouclé skirt and dove-gray jacket were much stuffier, Upper East Side old-money than Rylan's younger, hipper downtown style.

"Of course," Paige said smoothly. "We'll get started as soon as Ms. Biscotti arrives. We're expecting her at any moment. In the meantime, let me introduce Francesca. She's Allegra's assistant, fashion muse, and second-in-command. Allegra always says she couldn't survive without her." Suddenly noticing Rylan staring at Charlie as if trying to figure out who he was and what he was doing there, Paige added, "And that's Charlie. Intern."

Charlie nodded, while Francesca responded to her introduction with a lilting "*Piacere*."

"You're Italian?" Mrs. Sinclare asked, obviously intrigued. "Such a lovely country. I've vacationed there many times."

"*Fantastico!*" Francesca exclaimed. "I hope you have managed to fit in my own lovely town of Napoli?"

"Of course! We loved it."

"Why don't we have Francesca take your measurements while we wait for Ms. Biscotti," Paige suggested. Rylan stood, and Emma carefully watched Francesca measure Rylan: waist, hips, bust, neck, hip-to-knee, arms.

As Francesca measured, she chatted easily with the Sinclares about the sights of Italy, but Emma didn't pay much attention. Her anxiety was spiking again. She shot a look at Paige, who appeared as cool as a linen sundress on a hot day.

As if on cue, Paige's phone rang. "Please pardon me," she said to the Sinclares. "I'd better take that. It could be Ms. Biscotti calling from downstairs." She picked up the phone. "Paige Young," she said into it. "Oh, hello! I see… mm-hmm…Well, it can't be helped, I'm sure they'll understand…"

Emma held her breath. Mrs. Sinclare was still chatting with Francesca about Italy, disregarding Paige's conversation. Rylan was looking around the office curiously. Would this ruse work?

After a moment Paige hung up. "I'm afraid I have some regrettable news," she announced. "Ms. Biscotti was suddenly called away on important business to Paris. It's her upcoming collection. A problem with the manufacturing, I think. She was calling from the airport. She hopes you'll understand and accept her apologies for not being able to make it today."

Mrs. Sinclare frowned. "Well, this is certainly unfortunate. I suppose we'll have to reschedule. When will she be back in the country?"

"She wasn't sure," Paige said. "It all depends on how long it takes her to straighten out the problem."

"I see. Then I suppose this isn't going to work out after all." Mrs. Sinclare picked up her handbag, which she'd plopped in the middle of Paige's desk. "Our party is only a few weeks away. We'll have to find another designer."

Rylan shook her head "No way! I want *this* designer to make my Sweet Sixteen dress."

"No need to give up yet, Mrs. Sinclare," Paige put in with an ingratiating smile. "Francesca brought along Ms. Biscotti's sketches. In fact, Ms. Biscotti just suggested that we talk over initial ideas today and take measurements, if that's all right with you. She said Francesca is wonderful and will take good care of you, and of course I said I'd be happy to help as well. Then Francesca will email all the information to Ms. Biscotti in Europe, and she can take it from there and create your daughter a one-of-a-kind signature dress."

Mrs. Sinclare looked unconvinced. Emma held her breath, afraid that this meeting—and the money she was already counting on to buy materials for the pop-up collection— would be over before it began.

"Mother," Rylan said through gritted teeth. "Please."

Mrs. Sinclare glanced at her daughter. "Fine," she said. "I suppose we can give it a try."

"Wonderful." Paige smiled, then turned and snapped her fingers. "Emma. Pass me Allegra's sketchbook, please."

Francesca was closer to the sketchbook, which was sitting on a small end table, but Emma leaped over and grabbed it before Francesca could reach for it. The last thing they needed right now was to have the contents explode all over the place again.

Paige laid the sketchbook on her desk and opened it. "As you can see, Ms. Biscotti has made some preliminary sketches," she told the Sinclares as they gathered around. "I think you'll love the direction she's thinking, Rylan."

"I totally do!" Rylan exclaimed as she leaned forward for a better look. "It's awesome. Exactly the kind of thing I was imagining after I saw her stuff on the site." Rylan lingered over each page.

Emma dared a tiny glance at Charlie. He grinned at her.

"Yes, Allegra is so talented, is she not?" Francesca cooed, peering at the sketches over their shoulders. "And this dress, it will be so flattering to you, *Signorina* Rylan!" Francesca was pointing at the simple, sashed party dress.

"Yes! That's my favorite." Rylan beamed. "This dress is perfect!"

"Really, Rylan? *That's* what you want to wear? I don't know," interrupted Mrs. Sinclare.

"There are several options for customizing the look." Paige stepped in and took control. Emma could have hugged her. She carefully laid out the fabric samples from the sketchbook. "Allegra wants to do a sash that contrasts, in terms of color and texture, with the dress fabric. The sash will be a stretchy satin, and the dress itself a soft and drapey jersey. Shall we talk color?"

Paige is a genius, Emma thought. I never could have pulled this off.

"With your blue eyes, Rylan," Paige continued. "I think this bold sapphire-blue sash would be stunning. And really striking against a black jersey dress." Paige held up the cobalt blue and black swatches. They were totally fabulous—made to go together. Rylan loved Paige's suggestion. Why shouldn't she? Paige was, after all, about as big a fashion expert as there was. Everything was going so well. Emma couldn't believe her luck.

And then Mrs. Sinclare cleared her throat.

"I don't like it," she pronounced.

"Take a look at some of these other choices," Paige urged, not even a little bit flustered. She spread out the samples Emma had lovingly chosen—satins in emerald green, electric fuchsia, syrupy gold.

Mrs. Sinclare barely glanced at them, immediately dismissing them with a wave of her hand. "No, no. These are garish," she insisted. She stood, as if to remind everyone who was the most important person in the room.

alligator

$1,000,000,000

"I know!" Mrs. Sinclare smiled, finally seeming pleased about something. She opened up her bazillion-dollar Bottega purse and whipped out a napkin. A napkin the color of hospital walls. Pale green with more than a tinge of gray. Rylan watched silently, still clutching the black and cobalt samples.

She's got to be kidding, Emma thought. She waited for someone to laugh or make a joke. No one did.

Even Paige looked taken aback. "Er, you mean you want the dress to be the color of that napkin?"

"Yes." Mrs. Sinclare waved the napkin in the air like a flag. "I can see it now. The dress shall coordinate perfectly with the table linens my party planner is using."

"That's the color of the napkins for my party?" Rylan shrieked. "Mom! I said I wanted green."

"This is green."

"No, it's not. That's hideous. Sort of like puke, only more boring. Besides, it'll totally wash me out." Rylan looked truly horrified.

"Rylan." Mrs. Sinclare stared icily at her daughter.

"Colette Hervé is the most sought-after party planner in the city, and she has created an absolute vision for your party in seafoam and oyster tones. I, myself, shall be wearing oyster."

"But—"

"No buts." Mrs. Sinclare held the napkin up to the weak winter sunlight trickling in through the window. "Seafoam. That's what Colette says Martha Stewart calls this color. Very tasteful, very sophisticated, very soft. Don't you all agree?"

"Of course, of course," Francesca cooed. "Pastels are very classic, *si, signora?*"

Mrs. Sinclare smiled approvingly at her. "I can see why you're Allegra's trusted assistant, my dear," she said. "You have excellent taste."

Emma felt frozen in horror. This couldn't be happening. This woman couldn't actually be suggesting she make Rylan's dress that totally cringe-worthy shade of the mold that grew on the bagels her mom kept on the counter too long. For one thing, it didn't work with the design. *At all.* Besides that, Rylan was right. With her hair and fair skin, a color like that would make her look washed out and horrible, no matter what the dress itself looked like. In fact, that grayish-green would make an international supermodel look like death.

She was sure Paige had to be thinking the same thing. But when she looked over, the editor's face was blank except for a polite smile.

"We'll let Ms. Biscotti know," she said. "I'm sure she can find a wonderful fabric in that color."

"I hope so." Mrs. Sinclare looked pleased with herself. "I totally trust Colette. You know of her, don't you?"

Paige shook her head ever so slightly.

"Oh, well, she's really quite amazing. Great with color. She says this pale shade of green will be the new neutral. Don't you think?"

"Mmm." Paige was still smiling.

"Now, let's talk about that sash," continued Mrs. Sinclare. Paige met Emma's eye for a second and gave her the smallest of shrugs.

"I hate it." And just like that, Mrs. Sinclare ruined Emma's perfect party dress.

Emma felt like someone—Mrs. Sinclare, actually—had punched her in the stomach. She had no choice but to watch in silent, helpless horror. Mrs. Sinclare wanted a scoop neck and three-quarter-length sleeves. She wanted a dress that was unlike anything Emma had sketched, unlike anything she had any interest in designing. And mostly, a dress that was not at all Allegra Biscotti.

Emma kept expecting Rylan to speak up, and at first she did. Sort of. She tried to veto her mother's idea and kept directing her mother back to the original sketch. She totally got what Emma was trying to do. Rylan understood that the dress was all about the sash.

"Mom, it's cool because it almost looks like a kid's party dress, but it's so sophisticated!"

Emma was thrilled—for a split second.

Then Mrs. Sinclare shot her daughter down. "What do you know about sophisticated? You're not even sixteen yet." After that, Rylan's protests grew progressively weaker and whinier until, by the end, she just sullenly slumped in her chair.

Emma was surprised. Was this really Rylan Sinclare, the girl who ruled the high school like a queen? The one who'd reduced her to a quivering mass of insecurity with one cutting remark at Holly's apartment?

"There," Mrs. Sinclare said at last, pushing the sketchbook back toward Paige. "Now I think we have something to work with. You'll be sure that Allegra gets all my notes, right? And I'll leave the napkin with you, as well."

"Wait, Mom," Rylan spoke up at last. "Shouldn't I get to decide whether I like your changes or not? I mean, I'm the one who's going to be—"

"Oh my, look at the time!" her mother exclaimed, never acknowledging Rylan. "I've got another appointment with Colette. I must go."

"I understand," Paige said. "I think this has been a very productive start. And, yes, Francesca will send Allegra your suggestions straight off. Francesca will be in touch soon to set up the first fitting."

"Fitting?" Rylan put in. "Hold on. I think we might need another design meeting. You know, meet Allegra? She might want to talk about my mother's, um, adjustments."

"Enough, Rylan," Mrs. Sinclare barked so sharply that Emma jumped. "Would you stop acting like a whiny child? We're already behind schedule thanks to that idiot maid's carelessness with your first dress. I don't need a teenage temper tantrum causing more delays."

She spun on her heel, grabbed her handbag off the desk, and swept out of the room. Everyone sat in stunned silence for a moment. Wow. *That* had been harsh. Emma chanced a quick look over at Charlie. He met her eye, raised an eyebrow, and smirked slightly.

"What's *your* problem?" Rylan demanded, catching the knowing glance between them.

"Um…" Emma began. She had no idea how to answer.

"Shut it, okay?" Rylan snapped. "I don't need to be judged by the nerd gallery."

"*Bontá mia!*" Francesca exclaimed sorrowfully. "*Signorina*, you mustn't say such things to our Emmita. After all, she is really—"

"It's quite all right," Paige interrupted loudly. "It's been a stressful meeting, and I'm sure Miss Sinclare just wants to be sure her *Allegra Biscotti* original is perfect."

Francesca's eyes widened. Emma bit her lip. So much for being discreet.

Luckily Rylan didn't seem to notice anything strange. She

was staring at the floor. Had Francesca's comment actually made her think about being nicer? Emma doubted it. Still, there was an odd expression on Rylan's face that Emma couldn't quite read.

"Whatever," Rylan muttered. "I just hope Allegra can make something out of the mess my mother just created." Without another word, she turned and hurried out of the office.

Emma silently hoped that Allegra could, too.

"Oh. My. *God*." Paige blew out a loud breath and then rounded on Francesca. "I can*not*, repeat, *not*, believe you almost just blew Allegra's secret!"

Emma shot a nervous look at the door. It had closed behind Rylan fewer than thirty seconds earlier. She hoped it was soundproof, or at least close to it.

"*Mi dispiace, signorina!*" Francesca exclaimed, looking crestfallen. "I cannot believe it either! When I heard that girl saying such things...But I swear to you, I shall do better from now on."

Emma tentatively reached for her sketchbook, afraid to see what Mrs. Sinclare had done to her dress. Charlie stood behind her.

"It's a Mama Sinclare original," he joked weakly. "As seen on discount racks everywhere. Available in disaster-at-sea green."

"How am I supposed to work with this?" Emma mumbled. "This isn't a dress. It's a nightmare."

Paige heard her and turned away from scolding Francesca.

"You're going to have to turn it into a dream come true, Emma," she said, her tone softening.

Emma sucked in her breath. *If Paige has sympathy for me, it must be* really *bad,* she thought.

"How am I supposed to do that?" Emma asked. "She turned this into a nondescript seafoam sack. It's going to make Rylan look like she's got mono or something—"

"Yeah. It's not like Rylan even likes the new design," Charlie put in.

"Look, I know the changes stink," Paige said. "But Mrs. Sinclare is paying the bills, which makes her the client—*not* Rylan."

"But Rylan is the one who's going to look horrible if I actually make what her mother wants," Emma protested.

"Read my lips. Rylan is not your client." Paige tapped the sketchbook with one fingernail. "You've just got to make this work, Emma. There's no room for prima donnas in this business. At least not until you're a big name, which Allegra is not. Yet."

"But she will be soon!" Francesca chirped. Her bright smile had returned. She'd obviously moved on from her near-gaffe.

Judging by the look on Paige's face, *she* hadn't yet. "Yes," she said icily. "Now if you two will excuse me, I think Francesca and I need to have a talk."

Emma and Charlie walked down the hallway toward the elevators. Emma was so distracted by what had just happened in Paige's office that this time she hardly registered the fact that she was walking through *Madison*'s halls.

"I can't believe this," she moaned. "How am I supposed to make the design work with those crazy changes? It's impossible."

Charlie shoved his hands in his jeans' pockets as he strode along beside her. "What's the big deal? Just make the ugly dress, rake in the cash, and move on with your life. It's not like anyone will remember that one hideous dress once they get a load of your fab new pop-up collection, right?"

"That's not the point." Emma paused and frowned. Actually, it sort of *was* the point. But only one of them. "This dress is supposed to be for Rylan's big day. How can I put her in something I know is going to make her look bad?"

As they passed the reception desk and turned into the elevator lobby, Charlie shot her a look of disbelief. "You're actually worried about *Rylan?* Seriously?" he said. "It's not like she'd think twice about humiliating you if it came to that. Or anyone else either. I heard that she once snapped a picture of a so-called friend after she'd been crying her eyes out over some guy. The girl looked all puffy and gross, and of course, Rylan mass emailed it with a snarky comment."

He punched the button on the elevator and then turned to face her. "Speaking of big mouths, how about that Francesca?

She definitely looks and sounds the part, but she got totally scary-close to spewing the truth back there."

"Don't worry. Paige is the most uptight of anybody about keeping Allegra's secrets. She'll watch Francesca. Besides, it's not like she'll have that many more chances to mess up. Like Paige said, all she has to do is record that voice-mail message, maybe make a phone call or two, and come to a couple of fittings with Rylan." Emma grimaced. "*If* I don't give up on this whole thing and run away from home before the first fitting."

Charlie grinned at her as the elevator doors slid open. "We're running away? Awesome. Can we go someplace warm?"

CHAPTER 7

SEAMLESS

StylePaige

Weekend Update: Sweet Holiday Treats

Dear Style Gazers,

Oh yes, it's that time of year: Decorated store windows, bustling boutiques, and shop, shop, shopping! Too bad I've spent all my money on my honey. (It's something scrumptious, but he's a faithful reader so I can't spoil the surprise!)

But, don't let an overused credit card ruin your holiday cheer, fellow fashionistas. Why? My dear readers ask me. *Madison* is sponsoring a must-see pop-up shop for Choice New Designers. And luckily for generous gift-givers (like me!), it's a look-only event—just enough eye candy to make the season extra sweet.

Stop by and check out the amazing designers: Mario Guo, Kelso and Kiku, Allegra Biscotti, C. Leveille, and Ashana.

If you ask me—and you obviously have—this talented

group will be featured in all the boutiques come spring...just in time for our holiday charges to be paid off.

See you there!
Paige Young

"Emma!" A young woman in her early twenties, with fringy black hair and a tape measure draped around her neck, grinned and waved, as Emma stepped into Allure Fabrics the next day. "Excellent you came today. We just marked down a bunch of stuff. I set aside a flannel for you. I know you were looking at flannels last time."

"Thanks, Nidhi." Emma hurried over to take a look. Nidhi was her favorite salesperson at the fabric shop. She'd recently graduated from fashion school herself and was working at Allure mostly for the employee discount. She knew that Emma had designer tastes and a discount-store budget and always tried to help her out.

Of course, today Emma's budget was a little bigger than usual. Okay, a *lot* bigger. She reached into the baggy pocket of her army-surplus pants, touching the credit card her father had given her that morning. That way she didn't have to wait for Mrs. Sinclare's check to arrive before buying the materials for her pop-up collection.

"But listen, that's not all." Nidhi's warm brown eyes sparkled as she leaned closer. "You'll never guess who was in here yesterday. You've heard of Kelso McKay, yeah?"

"Um, sure." Emma had definitely heard of Kelso McKay. He was half of the design team of Kelso and Kiku, one of the other collections being featured in the pop-up shop.

Nidhi swept her bangs to the side. "Well, he must've spent two hours here. Supercool guy! He needed to find the perfect fabric for a jacket they're making for this pop-up shop *Madison* magazine's putting on soon. Do you know about it? Paige Young has been blogging about it all week.

"Most of Kelso's collection's been done for ages, of course. But he was, you know, fine-tuning things and decided he just had to add this one last piece. So I helped him find this super new organic cotton we just got in, and guess what? He invited me to come to the pop-up shop on opening day and meet Kiku. He even said they might be looking for a design assistant soon and I seemed perfect! Isn't that amazing?"

"Totally amazing," Emma said. And she meant it. But she had to do her best to keep her expression normal because her heart was pounding so fast.

She was dying to blurt out that *she* was making a collection for the pop-up, too. She knew the two of them would have a blast picking out fabrics together. But no, she had to keep the secret or Paige would kill her. She had to play it cool.

"This flannel *is* pretty great," she said, setting the remnant on the cutting table. It was a toffee and chocolate flannel, much cooler than the scraps Emma had been playing with. It would be perfect for the panels and sleeves on Holly's pink velvet dress. Emma thought about adding a little flannel Peter Pan collar as well.

"I'll take it. And I also need a few other things today." Hearing that other designers were putting the finishing touches on their collections while she'd barely started hers was threatening to send her into super-panic mode. She'd feel better once she had the fabric she needed.

"Hit me," Nidhi said. "What can I find you?"

Emma reached into her coat pocket and touched the folded list she'd stuck in there, though she didn't bother pulling it out. She'd looked at it so many times—adding, deleting, changing—that she had it memorized.

"I need something in bright candy colors. I'm thinking cotton candy, gumballs, swirly lollipops. Silky but with some weight."

"Sorry, cutie." Nidhi shook her head. "Nothing like that on the bargain table. How about a blend? Close enough, yeah?"

FIND
SWIRLY
FABRICS

"Not really." Emma cleared her throat. "Maybe I should take a peek at the full-price choices."

Nidhi looked surprised. "You sure? That stuff's pricey."

Emma nodded. "I'm sure."

"You'd better watch it, or you'll lose the title of my best bargain shopper," Nidhi joked. She turned and strode off toward the back of the store, speedy and sure-footed despite her four-inch wedges. "This way, yeah?" she called over her shoulder. "I guess if you're going to spend all your pennies on something, what I've got in mind is worth it."

As soon as she saw the gorgeous, subtly swirly, totally candy-colored silk Nidhi pulled out, Emma knew that it was perfect. "I'll take four-and-a-half yards, please," she said. One baby-doll mini down, thought Emma.

"Now I need a bunch of accordian-pleated silk. I want three colors that work together, but I'm torn between a citrony color scheme and a burnt orange." Leaving Nidhi to pull bolts down for her from the packed shelves, Emma wandered down the aisle. She hesitated at a section dominated by pale shades of green and ecru but kept going, not ready to deal with that just yet. First, the fun stuff. The disaster of a party dress could wait.

After running her fingers over the sumptuous pleated silks Nidhi had laid out, rolling the bolts around and mixing it up on a big scale, she decided on burnt orange, pomegranate, and lime green for the tiers of the princess dress. The top would be a stretchy gold knit she stumbled onto while she was roaming the aisles. She took generous cuts of each of the fabrics, so she could play around with the layering and add more if she liked.

Next, she wanted to get what she needed for *her* version of the simple party dress. Even though Mrs. Sinclare didn't like it, Paige had certainly sold Emma on the sapphire blue and black color combo. With Nidhi's help, Emma found a gorgeous, shiny, stretchy satin in a blue so rich that it practically sparkled and the softest, drapiest black jersey in the sale section. Again, she bought more than she needed of both. Since she wouldn't have time to make muslins of her designs—"practice" dresses using cheap fabric—she had to have some room for error.

Shopping without worrying about her budget was starting to make her feel better about Rylan's dress after all, so she decided to tackle that next.

Emma knew that she would *have to* find a way to deal with Mrs. Sinclare's changes. The seafoam green was horrible, but maybe Emma could just get the color a tiny bit wrong. Maybe she could edge it toward a pale turquoise. She looked for something shimmery—something that could possibly, in the right greenish light, pass for seafoam. And with Nidhi's help, naturally, she found it: an iridescent turquoise-green. The beautiful stepsister of Mrs. Sinclare's seafoam. It was worth a shot.

Each time Emma made a selection, Nidhi's left eyebrow arched a little higher, matching the growing height of the pile she was collecting for Emma on her cutting table.

"You sure about this one?" Nidhi asked, pausing with her shears poised to slice into the iridescent un-seafoam. "I might be able to find you something similar a little cheaper."

"That's okay. I really need this one." Emma could tell that Nidhi was curious but too polite to ask what was up. She wished again that she could tell her the truth. "Um, my dad's giving me an early birthday present."

Nidhi gave her a strange, searching look. "Happy birthday," she said at last. "Need anything else today?"

"Just some trimmings and stuff. I'll go get them."

"Okay. I'll start ringing up this stuff up front, yeah? It's going to take a while."

She gathered the pile as Emma hurried over to the trimmings wall, feeling elated and guilty at the same time.

Rolls of thread made an exquisite rainbow. Emma gathered an armful—cupcake pink, burnt orange, pomegranate, gold, lime, turquoise. The button section was dizzying, organized by color, and then by size and shape within each color section. It took Emma nearly fifteen minutes to find exactly what she was looking for—a package of tiny, pink crystal buttons for Holly's smock-dress makeover.

By the time Emma reached the counter with an armful of zippers, buttons, and thread, Nidhi had wrapped and rung up the fabric. She sorted expertly through the notions, adding them to the total. Then she ripped off the receipt and handed it to Emma. Emma gulped. The bill was more than she'd ever spent on fabric before. *Way, way* more.

But it was still less than what Mrs. Sinclare was paying for Rylan's dress. Pulling out her father's credit card, she handed it over. She had never used a credit card before.

Nidhi took the card and glanced at it. "Noah Rose," she read. "Your dad?"

"Uh-huh."

Nidhi bit her lip, shooting her a sidelong glance. "Sorry, cutie," she said, sounding a little embarrassed. "I'll need to call him for permission to let you use it. Store policy, yeah?"

Emma's father had warned her that this might happen. Even so, her cheeks went hot. "No problem," she mumbled. "Dad said to call his cell if there was a problem."

Soon Nidhi was speaking to Noah. "Thanks, sir," she said after listening for a moment. "I figured it was okay, but I had to check. Store policy." She listened for another few seconds and then burst into laughter. "No way, you can't pin this on me!" she exclaimed. "Your daughter has the fashion bug. Bad. She'd spend just as much time and money here if I'd never met her, yeah?"

Emma smiled weakly. Typical Dad. He loved to goof around with her friends, even ones he'd never met in person.

Nidhi traded a few more joking remarks with him and then hung up. "Sorry about that," she told Emma. "Ever since some first-year fashion-school twit swiped her mom's ATM card and emptied her account, Abe is super-paranoid about checking stuff. Especially when it's, um, a larger order." She shot a meaningful look at the overstuffed bags sitting on the counter.

"It's okay," Emma said, feeling more uncomfortable by the second under Nidhi's frank, friendly gaze. "I understand."

Nidhi quickly finalized the sale and then handed the credit card back to Emma. "So you making some good stuff with all this?" she asked. "I'd love to see how it turns out, yeah?"

It was a casual comment, just small talk, really. But Emma could hear the curiosity behind the words. She bent over the sales slip, quickly signing her name.

"Sure," she said. "Thanks again for everything, Nidhi." She gathered up her bags and scooted for the exit, fearing that if she didn't get out of there, she'd break down and tell Nidhi everything. And she couldn't do that. Even if it was difficult sometimes to remember why.

CHAPTER 8

CLOTHES ENCOUNTER

W hat are you doing?" William stuck his head into her room on Sunday after lunch.

Emma glanced up, startled, her body wrapped in a length of the stretchy black jersey. Her new fabrics covered every surface of her room so that she could see them all at once. Get to know them. See how they draped and stretched and moved.

"What does it look like?" she replied, scrunching the material. She wondered if she should cut this dress on the bias.

"It looks like you're playing girly-girl dress-up." William pranced around in a little circle, fluttering his fingers.

Emma rolled her eyes. "Did you want something? Or did you just stop by to annoy me?"

"I just stopped by to annoy you." He grinned and took off before she could respond.

She sighed, dropping the jersey on her bed. As tempting as it was to play with her new pop-up shop fabrics all day, she realized she couldn't. She'd barely looked at Rylan's dress—Mrs. Sinclare's redesigned version of it—since Friday's meeting. It was time to face the horror.

Gathering up the fabric hanging over her desk and chair, Emma sat down and flipped her sketchbook open. Mrs. Sinclare's changes were still there. And still bad. But as Paige had said, Emma was going to have to make it work. Somehow.

She started sketching, incorporating the woman's notes as best she could. Maybe she could make that scoop neck work. It wasn't the ideal proportion. Maybe she could move it up a notch so it was more of a low crew neck. The problem was that nothing worked without the sash...

Her phone buzzed, and she grabbed it. It was a text from Holly.

scoop?

less pouf

totally plain

> Hey Em! wuzup? want 2 hit a
> movie 2day?

Emily quickly texted back.

> Sorry. 2 busy. Some other time?

There was no response for a moment. Then the phone rang. Emma picked it up.

"Too busy?" Holly's familiar voice exclaimed. "No way. Nothing could be more important than seeing that new movie with the cute guy from that hot reality show. It's playing on 59th Street, and there's a discount matinee. Maybe we could get a hot chocolate or something after."

Emma doodled a sleeve design on a blank sheet. If Mrs. Sinclare wanted three-quarter length, would clingy and fitted work best? Or a flowy kimono sleeve? Or a fitted sleeve with a flowy cuff? Was it close enough to satisfy her? She was so distracted that it took her a second to realize what Holly was saying. Movie. Hot chocolate. Now.

"Sorry, I just *can't* today," Emma said.

"You sure? We can even swing by Bloomie's if you want," Holly pleaded. "I mean, I know we have that English test on Tuesday, and you're supposed to be grounded, but—"

"Sorry," Emma said again. "Not today. Maybe another time, okay? Look, I've got to go. I'll see you in school tomorrow."

"Okay. Bye." Holly sounded surprised.

Emma knew she didn't have time for *anything* until she figured out how she was going to make this dress look great.

By the time she trudged through the school doors the next morning, raindrops dripping off her yellow rubber boots,

Emma still hadn't figured it out. She'd sketched every possible version of Mrs. Sinclare's vision, but every sketch came out looking just as awkward as the next. What was she going to do?

Usually Emma loved a fashion challenge. Her favorite subway game was picking different pieces worn by her fellow riders and turning them into fabulous outfits in the pages of her sketchbooks. There was nothing she liked better than finding a vintage piece in a thrift shop and figuring out how to pair it with newer stuff to make it look trendy and current.

But this was different. How was she supposed to bring someone else's vision to life, especially when that person had no…taste? Above all else, fashion was supposed to be beautiful.

She was so lost in thought that she bumped into someone standing in the Downtown Day stairwell. "Oh, sorry," she mumbled, glancing up as she prepared to step around.

Then she saw that it was Jackson.

"Hey," he said with his casual half-smile.

"Um, hi!" she blurted out. "Sorry. I was just, you know, thinking about something. Really hard."

"It's cool." He shrugged. "I get that way sometimes."

"Cool." Emma smiled tentatively.

He nodded. They stood there for a moment, neither of them saying anything.

It should have been another awkward moment. Only it sort of…wasn't.

"Yo, Creedon!"

The shout broke the spell. Emma glanced back and saw several of Jackson's soccer buddies loping toward them. In the lead was Clayton Vanderbeck, a big, beefy guy with a blond buzz cut and the world's loudest voice.

"What's up, dude?" Clayton bellowed. "Been looking all over for you."

A skinny guy named Takumi eyed Emma up and down. "Yeah," he said to Jackson. "Guess you were busy."

The others snorted with laughter. Emma felt a flush of annoyance. Typical. Why did Jackson hang around with these jocks?

"I'm coming," Jackson mumbled, biting his lip in that super-cute way of his. He glanced at Emma as he headed up the stairs with the others. "See you."

"Bye," she said, though she doubted he could hear her over Clayton's guffaws.

She watched Jackson disappear around the corner of the landing and then sighed. She had no idea what to think. Then again, he'd said less than ten words to her, so there was probably nothing to think. Especially since he was still

Lexie's boyfriend. Maybe Holly can make sense of it, Emma hoped, as she hurried to her locker. The first bell was about to ring.

"Hi," Emma said.

Holly whirled around at the sound of her voice. "I just heard something fascinating over breakfast this morning," Holly announced with a frown, not bothering to return the greeting. "My sister told me that you're an intern for some hot, new fashion designer, Allegra Biscotti, who's designing Rylan's Sweet Sixteen dress."

Emma froze.

"Is it true?" Holly demanded, crossing her arms over her chest and glaring at Emma, her blue eyes flashing with anger. "Because I told Jennifer it couldn't possibly be. If my *best friend* had landed a cool gig like that, I would definitely know all about it. Right?"

Emma opened her mouth, but no sound came out. Her mind was spinning. She couldn't believe this was happening.

But duh. How could it not? Everything Rylan Sinclare did was big news for the Downtown Day gossip mill. And Jennifer was one of her best friends. Of course Holly was going to find out. Emma had been an idiot to think otherwise.

"I'm sorry," she blurted out. "I should have—I mean, I guess I—I mean…" Her words faltered as the anger in Holly's eyes turned to hurt.

"So it's true?" Holly said. "That's why you've been blowing me off lately?" She shook her head. "Why didn't you tell me?"

Why *hadn't* she? Good question. And suddenly Emma couldn't think of a single good answer. Holly was her best friend. She had a right to know. *Everything*.

"Listen, Holls," she began.

"Holls!" someone squealed. "OMG, did you ask her? Is it true?"

Emma hardly had time to recognize Kayla's voice when suddenly Ivana and all her Bees were swarming around them. "Holly—" Emma began again.

"Apparently it's true," Holly told Ivana and the others, her voice ice cold. "Guess the joke's on me."

"Bummer." Ivana shot Emma a curious, calculating look. "But don't beat yourself up, Holls. It *is* pretty hard to believe."

"H-Holly, listen," Emma stammered. "I—I meant to tell you. It's just, it's kind of complicated…"

"You got a job." Holly shrugged, not meeting her eye. "What's so complicated about that?"

Emma cast a desperate look at Ivana and her friends. If only they weren't here, she'd just forget her promise to Paige and tell Holly everything. About Allegra and *Madison* and the pop-up collection and all the rest. That was the only chance to fix this.

But she couldn't. Not with sharp-eared Ivana and the Bees hanging around, drooling for juicy gossip. How could she make Holly understand that she'd never meant to hurt her?

"Can we go somewhere and talk about this?" she begged. "Please?"

"There's nothing to talk about. I mean, it's obvious I don't count in your life anymore." Holly slammed her locker door shut. "Later, Emma."

Emma stood there helplessly as Holly walked away with Ivana and the Bees.

CHAPTER 9

TRENDING DOWN

Emma tapped her purple lace-up boot impatiently as Ms. MacMaster droned on and on. Something about descriptive words in the first-person narrative, although she wasn't really listening. She'd spent the entire English class trying to catch Holly's eye.

Normally, that wasn't hard in this class. Holly sat right across the aisle. She usually entertained herself by making funny faces at Emma anytime the teacher's back was turned. Mostly to keep them both awake.

But not today. Today she was staring straight ahead, eyes on the board, doing a fairly good impression of someone who found the correct usage of pronouns and adjectives utterly fascinating.

Emma glanced down at the sketchbook in her lap. If she couldn't get Holly's attention, maybe at least she could get some work done on the dress design. But when she put her pencil to the paper, it refused to move. What was the point? She couldn't make a dress out of Mrs. Sinclare's—or anyone's—requirements. Maybe she wasn't meant to be a designer. Designers must have to deal with clients all the time.

She glanced around the classroom, hoping for inspiration. Most of the class looked just as excited as she was about today's lecture. They were yawning, snoozing, or staring blankly into space. All except one person. Ivana. She sat right behind Holly, her cool, calculating eyes trained on Emma.

Emma blushed and spun around to face front again. This wasn't the first time she'd caught Ivana staring at her today. Ever since she'd found out about Emma's "internship," Emma seemed to have gone from completely invisible to the number-one object of Ivana's attention. What was that about? Emma didn't know, but it was one more wrinkle she definitely didn't need.

Charlie held out a hand to stop Emma before she could step past the filing cabinets into her studio. "Wait," he ordered. "Before you go in, I'm officially declaring this a No Angst Zone."

"A what?" Emma stared at him.

"You can't let this Holly stuff throw you off," Charlie said.

"You've got a ton to do, and it's too important to risk it all over your latest meltdown."

Emma frowned. "My friendship with Holly is important, too. Way important," she argued.

"Look. You can't fix this thing with Holly until she stops being so mad."

"Do you think she will?" Charlie had known Holly for almost as long as she had.

"She will." Charlie paused. "Eventually."

Emma hoped Charlie was right. She didn't want to think about any other possibilities.

"And you'll deal with it then. Right now, focus on designing." Charlie grinned at her. "Deep cleansing breath?"

Emma inhaled deeply and then blew his face. "How's that?"

Charlie wrinkled his nose. "Smells like barbecue potato chips," he said. "But it'll do."

When they stepped into her studio, Emma nearly tripped over the bulging shopping bags filled with the fabrics she'd bought at Allure. "Dad brought everything here!" she exclaimed. "Wait until you see what I got."

Charlie peeked into the first bag. "Brown flannel?" he asked. "Are you making pajamas?"

"The brown flannel is going to be worked into this

pink velvet dress," she said, motioning to the dress already adorning the dress form, "to transform it into a fabulous grown-up-sized smock dress. But that'll have to wait. I need to figure out what to do about Rylan's dress."

"What do you need me to do?" Charlie asked.

Emma glanced at him. This new, helpful Charlie was kind of weird, but why not go with it? "I guess you could unpack those bags and organize the fabric and other stuff so it's ready to go," she said. "Most of the pop-up sketches are in my sketchbook. If you check the notes in the margins, you should be able to figure out which fabrics and notions go with which pieces."

Charlie grabbed a notebook out of the small stack on the worktable and flipped it open. "This chicken scratch?" he said, peering at the page. "What's 'jersey' mean?"

"It's the cotton jersey—that black kind of knit fabric." Emma shrugged. "Just do your best."

As Charlie dug into the first bag, Emma forced herself to turn away and sit at the worktable with the Rylan sketch. Opening it to the page with Mrs. Sinclare's notes, she stared at it for a long moment, wishing she could just make the original dress instead—the one both she and Rylan loved. It would be so easy. Rylan would have a great dress to wear to her Sweet Sixteen, and Emma could go back to focusing on the pop-up collection, knowing she'd created something beautiful.

But no. Mrs. Sinclare was the client, at least according to Paige. Emma had to find some way to make her happy. What would Allegra Biscotti do? she wondered. If she was a worldly-wise hot designer, she would…

"What's all the noise?" Charlie asked, looking up from a pile of zippers and thread.

Emma pushed away her sketchbook and stood. "Let's go see."

In the reception area, Marjorie was on her feet, doing her best to stare down the impossibly tall, impossibly gorgeous figure wrapped in a long coat of sand-colored cashmere, rising on five-inch stilettos and with flowing hair held back from her face with a sparkly dragonfly-shaped clip.

"Francesca?" Emma blurted out.

"What's *she* doing here?" Charlie whispered.

Emma ignored Charlie's goofy half-smile and shook her head. Francesca turned and spotted them.

"Emmita!" she cried. Sweeping over, she grabbed Emma's face in her hands and planted a kiss on each cheek. "I was just explaining to your front-desk lady that I am here to work for Allegra."

Marjorie looked anxious. "I was just trying to tell this, er, lady that Allegra isn't here at the moment."

"Believe it or not, it's okay, Marjorie. Francesca knows *all* about Allegra. We met at *Madison*."

"Yes, that is correct." Francesca beamed at Emma as she finished. "*Signorina* Paige, she has now sent me over to do whatever you need from me." She glanced around the reception area. While slightly more refined than the rest of the warehouse, it was far from *Madison*'s luxe waiting room. Francesca scrunched up her nose in obvious distaste.

"This place, it is charming in its own way. Like something from one of your American movies!" Francesca declared.

"Like Freddie Krueger's world in *A Nightmare on Elm Street*?" Charlie joked.

"Never mind," Emma put in. She wasn't sure quite what she was supposed to do with Francesca. "Maybe you can start by recording that voice-mail message?" she suggested. She glanced at Charlie. "Can you take her somewhere to do that? Maybe the showroom. It's quieter and less echoey in there than anywhere else in this place."

"Of course," Charlie said without taking his eyes off the Italian beauty. "Come with me, Francesca. I'll grab the phone, and we'll do this thing."

The two of them disappeared down the narrow hallway, Francesca's cheery chatter fading away as they went. Marjorie shook her head.

"This is an interesting turn of events," she said. "What's someone like that supposed to do around here?"

"Um, I'm not sure," Emma admitted. "I'd better go call Paige and find out."

Marjorie nodded, looking ready to say something else. But at that moment the phone rang. Emma hurried back to her studio. Grabbing her cell, she quickly dialed Paige's number.

"Um, Francesca's here, and—" she began uncertainly when Paige answered.

"Thank God, she made it," Paige broke in. "I swear, that girl could get lost in a studio apartment. Not to mention being hopeless with a coffee order."

"Okay," Emma said. "So what am I supposed to do with her?"

"But that was the plan." Paige sounded surprised. "Weren't you paying attention? We're killing three birds with one stone here, remember?"

"Which birds exactly? I mean, I know we needed her to help out with that meeting—"

"Right, that's number one," Paige said. "Number two, she's a handy public face for Allegra Biscotti whenever else we might need her—for voice mail, client phone calls, whatever. Number three, if she's over there working for you, she ceases to be a problem for me here, *without* alienating her father and risking him pulling his advertising from the magazine. Which would be *mucho no bueno*, if you catch my drift."

114

"Yeah." Emma didn't bother pointing out that she was rather sure that last part was Spanish, not Italian. "But does she think this is, like, a real job? Because I don't really have any money for an assistant or anything."

Paige laughed. "Don't worry. You don't have to pay her," she said. "Just treat it as an unpaid internship for now. Francesca doesn't need the money. Her family is loaded. Like, Arab-sheik loaded, practically. No, she just wants to feel like she's part of the New York fashion world. This way, she does that, you get a little free help, and *Madison* stays in one piece. Win-win-win."

"I guess that makes sense," Emma said.

"Good. Listen, I just got called into a meeting. Talk later."

"Bye," Emma said, though she was pretty sure Paige had already hung up.

She stood there for a second staring at her phone. Maybe Paige was right. Emma already knew she'd never be ready for the pop-up opening in time without leaning on Marjorie's help with construction and sewing. Maybe Francesca could share that load. Paige had mentioned that Francesca had some fashion-school training, right?

"Emmita!" Francesca burst into view. She'd taken off her coat somewhere along the way, revealing a figure-hugging mauve cashmere skirt with a cashmere T-shirt in a barely darker shade of mauve tucked in, and a wide, still darker mauve suede belt wrapped around her teeny, tiny waist. "Is this your studio? It is so charming!"

Charlie followed and tossed the Allegra phone back to Emma. "Message done," he said. "Most of it's even in English."

"Thanks." Emma set the phone down beside her other one. "Listen, Francesca. If you really want to stick around and help—"

"Oh, I do!" Francesca clasped her hands together, making her armful of heavy bangle bracelets clink. Emma wondered if they were real gold. Probably, considering what Paige had told her.

"Okay, cool," Emma said. "I need to work on some sketches right now. While I'm doing that, maybe you could finish unpacking and sorting the fabrics I just bought for the collection."

"Hey!" Charlie protested. "I was doing that."

Emma shot him a surprised look. She'd expected him to be glad to be relieved of fabric-sorting duty, but he actually looked put out. And an annoyed Charlie was an *annoying* Charlie, as she knew from previous experience.

"I know," she said, thinking fast. "But, um, I was hoping you could do it *together*."

He grinned. Emma thought he looked ridiculous and made a mental note not to leave the two of them along for too long.

"Charlie? Please would you fetch me some water with gas? Or how do you Americans call it? Bubbles? *Grazie!*" Francesca chirped. "With a hint of fresh lime." She dumped one of the shopping bags onto the worktable, almost knocking over Emma's water bottle.

Charlie caught it just in time and set it aside atop a filing cabinet. "Gassy water it is. Em? Chips and soda all right for you?"

"Fine. Thanks."

Charlie hurried out; Francesca turned her attention to the fabrics, humming under her breath as she started sorting them; and Emma went back to work. The party-dress design frustrated her every time she looked at it. She knew how perfect the original dress she'd designed would look on Rylan. Actually, it would look great on anyone with its totally simple lines and flirty skirt and, mostly, the amazing sash that turned it into different dresses based on how you tied it all up, like a present.

With Mrs. Sinclare's changes? Not so much.

"Aargh!" Emma exclaimed as she crossed out yet another

attempt to make the new and not-so-improved design work.

"What is it, Emmita?" Francesca looked up from folding a piece of soft dove-gray flannel.

"Just this stupid design," Emma said with a sigh. "I can't get it right. I wish I could just make the dress I want to make."

"Let me see." Francesca hurried toward the stool where Emma was sitting while she sketched. As she did, her hip brushed against one of the dress forms. It toppled over with a crash. "Oops!" Francesca said with a giggle. "*Mi scusi*, I am so clumsy when distracted."

"It's okay." Emma quickly righted the dress form. When she turned around, Francesca was peering at the dress sketch.

"What is so troublesome to you, Emmita?" she asked. "This dress, it is *molto bello*."

Emma shook her head, assuming from Francesca's tone and expression that *molto bello* was a compliment. "No, it isn't. You don't have to be polite." She hurried over and flipped back to the original design. "This is the dress I want to make."

"Oh, it is beautiful!" Francesca exclaimed. "You are so talented, *bella mia!*"

"Thanks. But—"

"Chow's here!" Charlie sang out, hurrying into the studio and dropping a couple of greasy bags onto the worktable.

Emma blanched. "Watch the fabric!" she cried, yanking the bags away from a gorgeous piece of silk and dumping them onto a folding metal chair on the far side of the studio instead. "You don't want me to have to forbid you from eating in here, do you?"

Charlie ignored her, digging into one of the bags. "That place we usually go to on 8th Avenue was closed, so I got fries from the truck on the same block."

Emma accepted the soda he handed her. Then he reached into the bag again. "No bubbly water, sorry," he told Francesca. "I got you a Diet Sprite."

"Diet? Eh, okay," Francesca responded, catching the soda as he tossed it to her.

"So how's it going?" Charlie asked Emma.

"I'm still stuck on Rylan's dress," Emma admitted.

"Really?" Leaving the snacks behind, Charlie stepped over for a look at the latest sketch. "Ouch! Yeah, I'm no Allegra Biscotti or anything, but that's not looking too hot to me. Still, if it's what Rylan's crazy mother wants, you should—hey!" he interrupted himself as there was a rustle from behind them.

Emma glanced back just in time to see Francesca squirting gobs of ketchup all over the fries Charlie had set out. "What is it?" Francesca asked, another packet poised to squeeze.

Emma looked at the ketchup, then fries, and then fabric—all side by side. Anxiety level = 10. She swallowed a giant gulp of air and tried to tune out potential disaster about to happen. She really needed to focus to get this design out of the way so she could go back to the fun pop-up stuff. Sinking onto the wooden stool, she began sketching yet again.

"How's it going back here?" Marjorie stuck her head into the studio a half hour later.

Emma glanced up from another failed attempt to mesh her vision with Mrs. Sinclare's. "So-so," she said. "Charlie hasn't killed Francesca yet, and she's only knocked over the dress form twice so far."

Marjorie looked amused. "Where are those two?"

"Francesca went to the bathroom for a mascara touch-up," Emma said. "Charlie's off getting himself some fries with no ketchup."

Marjorie nodded and walked over to glance at Emma's sketchbook. "And you? How are you doing?"

"Not so hot." Emma rubbed her temples. "This design is making me nuts!"

"Tell me." Marjorie perched on the next stool.

So Emma did. She outlined the whole Rylan project, including the meeting and Emma's problems incorporating Mrs. Sinclare's notes into the design. Marjorie nodded sympathetically through all of it.

"That's a tough seam to sew," the receptionist said at the end. "And you're right, by the way. That woman has no eye whatsoever if she thinks those comments will work in any way with your lovely design." She cast a dismissive glance at the sketchbook and the napkin now tacked to Emma's inspiration wall. "But you can't change people or their personal taste—or lack thereof." She shrugged. "All you can do is be true to yourself, trust your instincts, and let the rest fall into place."

"Yeah." Emma thought about that. "I guess you're right."

She stared at her sketch. Suddenly she knew what to do.

CHAPTER 10

NEWS OF THE DAY

T his can't be right," Emma muttered a couple hours later. She pulled out the pin she'd stuck through the muslin pattern piece.

"Huh?" Charlie glanced up from the comic book he was reading. "Did you say something?"

"I said this can't be right." Emma frowned, adjusting the muslin pieces and trying again. "It's not hanging right at all."

After her conversation with Marjorie, she knew that what she desperately wanted was to make the dress she'd originally designed. To bring it to life. It would be a crime not to. She'd made a point of checking out Rylan's outfit every day since she'd found out that she would be designing her Sweet Sixteen dress. And every day, Rylan wore something black. Black was her neutral. Emma couldn't put Rylan in seafoam. But maybe there was a way to make Rylan happy without making her mother too, too mad.

Maybe Emma could go back to her original design *and* be true to herself. Give Mrs. Sinclare her three-quarter-length sleeves and her scoop neck. But *keep* the sash that made the dress a true Allegra Biscotti. She could use the pretty iridescent turquoise that could maybe pass for seafoam for the sash. After all, *she* wasn't going to be explaining herself to Mrs. Sinclare. That would be up to Francesca. Or Allegra calling in from Paris.

Not wanting to waste any more time, she'd gone straight to cutting a muslin pattern. Now she wondered if she'd worked too fast.

Charlie stood, stretched, and wandered closer. "Humor me here," he said. "Pretend I'm just some guy who doesn't know anything about, you know, sewing and fashion and stuff. What are you talking about?"

Emma fiddled with the muslin on the dress form and scrunched her nose. "Can't you see it doesn't look right? It's not just that Mrs. Sinclare ruined the design. This pattern doesn't look like it'll fit Rylan at all!"

Charlie seemed underwhelmed by the news. "So what's the big deal?" he said. "Francesca must've measured something wrong. That's not so shocking, is it?"

Emma bit her lip. "Maybe you're right. I *hope* you're right."

Stepping over to the worktable, she checked the measurements Francesca had written down during the meeting. They were just as she'd thought. Just as she'd carefully patterned.

Charlie returned his attention to his comic book. Hurrying past him, Emma headed for the reception area.

"Do you have a sec?" Emma asked Marjorie. "I need another set of eyes."

"Sure, honey."

Marjorie circled the dress form with a critical gaze. "Unless your school friend is shaped like Godzilla, something is definitely off in the numbers here," she announced.

Emma's heart sank. She was hoping Marjorie would catch something she'd missed. Some fudged measurement or mismatched seam that would explain the weird shape of the muslin garment. When Marjorie left to return to her post, Emma stared at the dress form in total dismay.

"Francesca must have measured wrong," she said. "Or maybe written the numbers down wrong. Where is she?" She glanced over at Charlie.

"Not sure. I sent her out on an errand." Charlie shifted his gaze away from hers, looking vaguely guilty.

"An errand? What kind of errand?"

"I might have told her you were a huge fan of this one specific kind of European candy bar," Charlie admitted. "And that the closest shop that has them is up in Midtown." He smiled weakly.

Emma gritted her teeth. "So now what am I supposed to do? These measurements are all wrong, and we're supposed to have a fitting this Friday afternoon!"

"Don't panic. We can totally fix this," Charlie said. "We'll just find Rylan at school tomorrow and tell her Francesca messed up and we need to re-measure. She'll totally believe it coming from Allegra's loyal interns, right?"

"Are you crazy?" Emma shook her head. "We can't do that. It's totally unprofessional."

Charlie pursed his lips. "You have a point," he admitted. "Allegra's rep definitely shouldn't suffer just 'cause Francesca's clueless. Okay, so we need another plan. I'll put my genius mind to work on it."

"You do that," Emma told him. "I'm texting Paige."

A minute later, the Allegra phone rang.

"Just got your text," Paige said, sounding distracted. Emma could hear her multitasking on her computer keyboard. "What's this about measurements?"

Emma told her. "I think Francesca made a mistake," she finished. "But she's not here right now, so I can't ask her."

"Nonsense. Even Francesca couldn't mess up something so basic," Paige said. "Isn't that kind of thing, like, lesson one in fashion school? You'd better double-check your measurements or whatever."

"I already did. Four times," Emma said. "And there's

just no way the waist length is even close to right, plus, the shoulders are—"

"Hold on," Paige broke in. "I'm an editor, not a seamstress, okay? I'm all about the finished product, not so much the sewing stuff. That's supposed to be your department."

Emma opened her mouth to protest but closed it without saying a word. "Okay," she said instead. "I, um, guess I'll go check again."

"Well?" Charlie said after she'd hung up. "What'd she say?"

"Not much. She thinks I just need to work it out."

Charlie shook his head. "How are you supposed to do that?"

"That's where you come in, right? I think it's time for one of your genius ideas."

StylePaige: Monday evening

Faithful readers of this blog already know all about the hot-hot-hot pop-up shop coming soon to the streets of SoHo, courtesy of *Madison* magazine. But here's the inside scoop from your fashion-first reporter. A little bird told me that Allegra Biscotti's new designs for the collection are more super-scrumptious than ever. They're sugar-and-spice and oh-so nice! Check it out for yourself, fellow fashionistas. Or check back here for all the glam deets—I'll be blogging live from the socialista scene.

"Hi, Holls," Emma said tentatively when she reached her locker on Tuesday morning.

Holly was bent over, digging a book out of her own locker. She straightened up and turned, managing to look at Emma without actually meeting her eye. "Hi," she said in a whiff of cherry-scented chewing gum.

Emma hesitated. Okay, at least Holly wasn't giving her the silent treatment anymore. But this wasn't much better.

"Um…" she began, trying to find the words to apologize, to convince Holly to give her another chance.

"Emma!" A girl with wildly curly blond hair and round, tortoise-shell glasses rushed toward her. Emma had a couple of classes with Abby Diehl, but as far as she could recall, they'd never spoken. "I just heard you're interning for Allegra Biscotti! How cool is that?"

Emma shot a desperate glance at Holly. But she was already halfway down the hall. Emma forced a smile. She sort-of remembered that Abby had a sister, or maybe it was a cousin, who was friendly with Rylan. Figured. "It's no big deal," she said. "It's just an after-school job."

For the rest of the day, Emma switched between being the

school's biggest celebrity and the world's worst friend. Holly continued to be polite but distant and sort of sad. Everyone else at Downtown Day couldn't get enough of Emma now that the word had spread that she and Charlie were Allegra's interns.

Of course, Emma was quite sure that about 99 percent of the kids at school had never heard of Allegra before now. But Rylan was a trendsetter who debuted the newest and hottest and most must-know things in the world to all her followers. Which included almost everyone at Downtown Day.

"Stupid gossipy school," Emma muttered to Charlie just before lunchtime. "Will you come to the caf with me?"

"No can do. I've got somewhere to be."

"Where?" Emma asked. Charlie often avoided the cafeteria, but she'd been hoping he'd make an exception today. Buddy system and all that.

cool banister

"Anywhere but there," he said.

"Wait!" Emma protested. But he was already gone.

She slowly walked down the stairs, momentarily fascinated by the symmetrical pattern made by the poles in the banister. She stopped and opened her sketchbook. Most of the students had already disappeared down to the basement cafeteria or into the student lounge by now, and the area was deserted.

Well, *almost* deserted. She gulped as she spotted Jackson coming toward her. Suddenly she forgot about color-blocking pole stripes and everything else. As he came closer, looking cuter than ever in a hunter-green hoodie that made the subtle highlights in his brown hair shimmer, it was all she could do to remember to breathe and keep standing upright.

"Hey," he said when he reached her. "What's up?"

"Not much," she said cautiously, closing her sketchbook.

"What are you drawing?"

"Just a pattern. Fashion stuff. What I usually draw." She wondered if he'd ask to see, since he liked to draw, too. But he didn't.

He nodded. "Lexie told me about your internship thing," he said.

"Yeah?" What else had Lexie told him?

"I never knew anyone our age who had a job like that."

Emma blushed. It sounded nice coming from him.

"Yeah," she said. "Thanks. I mean, it is kind of cool, I guess." She could feel a flushed heat on her cheeks. He was smiling at her, and she smiled back.

The moment was cut short by the clatter of someone coming down the steps. Emma glanced back and spotted a pair of feet in cute jeweled-toe flats. Then she looked up and saw that they were attached to Ivana.

"Oh, hello," Ivana said, stopping short and surveying the two of them with interest. "Jackson, aren't you supposed to meet Lexie in the caf?"

"Right. Um, see you guys later." Without another glance at Emma, Jackson turned and raced down the stairs.

Emma made a move to head in the same direction, but Ivana's cool voice stopped her. "So," Ivana said, her peach-glossed lips turning up in a slight smirk. "Keeping secrets isn't nice, you know. Especially from your so-called best friend."

"Thanks for the advice." Emma was careful to keep her voice steady, not wanting Ivana to know she was intimidated by her. "I'll keep it in mind."

"You do that." Ivana studied her face. "So how'd you land a gig like that, anyway?"

"Oh, you know," Emma said vaguely. "My dad works in the Garment District, and he knows a few people…"

"Hmm. So how long have you been working for Allegra? I mean, nobody ever even heard of her until almost five minutes ago." Ivana's gaze wandered down to Emma's jeans, gray cardigan, and silver sneakers. "I'm sort of surprised she found interns so fast."

Emma was fairly sure that wasn't actually what Ivana was thinking. She was wondering how the girl she'd been completely ignoring for, oh, the past zillion years had ended up working with a new designer before Ivana herself had even heard of her. That had to sting, and Emma allowed herself a small quiver of satisfaction.

"So what's she like?" Ivana went on, her bored tone of voice trying to convey that she didn't really care that much about the answer, though her sharp, probing eyes said otherwise. "Do you actually have anything to do with her, or are you mostly, like, answering the phone or whatever?"

"Oh, no!" Emma said, feeling suddenly spirited. "I work *very* closely with Allegra on just about everything. She's the best boss ever. Makes me really feel like a part of the creative process, you know? She really values my input. In fact, sometimes it almost seems like the two of us have the exact same, you know, style."

Okay, that had been kind of mean, but also fun. Charlie must be rubbing off on her.

But she had to give it to Ivana—she stood as unwavering as a statue with that ever-present smirk plastered on her face.

Emma's smile faded as she spotted Holly heading toward the student lounge. "I've got to go," Emma said, pushing past Ivana, darting around the corner, and breaking into a jog. She caught up to Holly right before she reached the lounge.

"Hey," Emma said breathlessly, putting out a hand to stop her. "Can I talk to you?"

Holly turned toward her, stone-faced. "It's a free country," she said tonelessly.

Emma took a deep breath, gathering her thoughts.

"Listen," she said, "I really want to explain about the whole Allegra thing. I was dying to tell you about it—you know I always tell you everything. I totally didn't mean to keep this from you."

Holly stared at her. Her blue eyes were guarded. Emma couldn't tell if her apology was getting through or not. Before she could continue, she heard a buzz from her sweater pocket.

She winced.

"Aren't you going to get that?" Holly said tonelessly as the muffled buzz came again.

Emma fumbled in her pocket and glanced at the caller ID for the Allegra phone. Another phone number she didn't recognize.

Holly turned away and walked off toward the lounge.

"Holly, wait!" she called.

But Holly didn't look back. In fact, she picked up speed.

Emma was tempted to chase her down. Holly might have longer legs, but Emma had always been able to run faster than her, ever since they were little kids.

The thought had barely crossed her mind when she shook her head, knowing it probably wouldn't do any good. Not when she still didn't know what to say to make this better. When she still couldn't tell Holly the whole truth.

The phone buzzed again. Angrily.

"Hello?" Emma said, answering the phone, her eyes and attention on Holly retreating.

"Hello? Is this, uh, Allegra Biscotti's office?" a familiar female voice asked.

"Yes, this is Emma," Emma said. "Who's this?"

"Emma?" the person sounded surprised.

"It's Rylan. I wasn't expecting *you* to answer. Aren't you, like, in school right now?"

Rylan? Rylan was calling Allegra?

Emma desperately wished she had let the phone go to voice mail. She paused to consider how weird it must seem for her to be picking up Allegra's phone at this time of the day.

"You there?" Rylan asked.

"Um, yeah," she said, thinking fast. "Allegra forwarded her phone to me because, uh, she's still in Europe."

"Okay." Rylan sounded dubious. "So why isn't Francesca answering?"

"Oh." Emma hadn't thought about that. There were a lot of pieces to this Allegra puzzle that she hadn't put together yet. "She—she had a dentist's appointment." She winced, belatedly realizing how stupid that sounded.

But miraculously, Rylan bought it. "Oh, okay," she said. "But I was really hoping to talk to Allegra, or at least Francesca."

"Maybe I can help?" Emma offered.

There was a long pause, and Emma wondered if Rylan had hung up.

"I don't know how you could possibly help me," Rylan said slowly. "I *really* need to talk to Allegra about my dress."

"Sorry. Like I said, she's in Europe."

"Right, I got you the first time. Last I heard they had phones over there, or am I missing something?" Rylan's voice was taking on a snippy tone. "So I need her to call me as soon as possible. Or she can email or text me. Whatever way."

"I'm afraid that probably won't work out." Emma wished Paige or Charlie was here to tell her what to say. "She's traveling around a lot, and so—"

"Look, I've never heard of anything so weird. If she can't even be bothered to call back an important client, maybe she's not the right designer for me after all," Rylan snapped. "Tell her to call me, or I'll tell my mother I changed my mind about the whole thing."

There was a click. She'd hung up.

Emma's mind was whirling. Her first reaction was to hope that Rylan would follow through on her threat to pull the project. Emma's life would be a lot easier without that party dress.

But then again, she'd already spent a huge chunk of the money Mrs. Sinclare was paying her. It wouldn't be fair to stick her parents with the bill. Besides, she didn't want to get Paige in trouble. It sounded as if Rylan's dad was a pretty big deal at *Madison*'s parent company.

She stared at the phone in her hand, realizing she now had two huge problems to solve.

"Where have you been?" Emma said as Charlie rushed into her studio that afternoon, out of breath and pink cheeked from the cold December wind outside. "I thought you only had to stay after for half an hour to retake that quiz."

Charlie flopped onto a stool and slung his bag onto the filing cabinets. "Sorry. Got hung up talking to Mike Harlow and those guys afterward. But I got here as fast as I could. What's the big emergency, anyway?"

Emma filled him in on Rylan's hysterics.

"Easy." Charlie shrugged off his worn, twilight-blue peacoat and reached out his hand. "Allegra phone, please."

Emma eyed him suspiciously.

"*Please.*"

Emma sighed and passed him the phone. He had that mischievous glint in his eye. Never a good sign.

Charlie flipped open the phone and started typing. When he was finished, he showed her the text message.

Ciao, Rylan! So sorry I was not there 2 meet u last week. But I am excited 2 make u the dress of ur dreams. Europe is the perfect inspiration for me, and I know u will be thrilled! Can't wait 2 meet u f2f soon. Peace & fashion, Allegra Biscotti.

"Peace and fashion?" Emma wrinkled her nose. "That doesn't seem like something Allegra would say."

"Well, what do you suggest? I didn't think XOXO or TTYL seemed very professional," Charlie said. "And I don't know how to say anything in Italian except *Ciao*, and I already used that at the beginning. Besides, lots of famous people have signature sign-offs."

"I guess it'll do." Emma took a deep breath and then hit send. There. Maybe that would be enough to keep Rylan happy, at least for now.

"Think she'll believe it's really from Allegra?" Charlie asked.

"I hope so. Maybe I'll ask Francesca to give her a call later, just to follow up."

Charlie made a sour face. "You sure that's a good idea? The girl is gorgeous but a total loose cannon. Or however you say 'loose cannon' in *Italiano*."

"I have another idea. I think Allegra should have a blog. It will help explain where she is and why she is too busy to see anyone." Emma's idea was partly inspired by StylePaige, which Emma had read faithfully since long before she'd known Paige.

"I'm all over that!" Charlie pulled his laptop out of his bag and immediately started it up. Once logged into the newly live Allegra Biscotti site, he began typing furiously. Then he tilted the laptop toward her. The brand-new blog's headline read: *Ciao from Allegra!*

"What do you think?" Charlie looked proud.

"Works for me."

"Now what?" Charlie poised his fingers over the keyboard.

"I figure if we create a diary of Allegra's European trip, maybe Rylan and her mom will be so impressed with all the important stuff she's doing over there that they won't complain too much when she doesn't show up for the next meeting either." Emma closed her eyes. If she were a worldly fashion designer jaunting across Europe, what would she blog about?

Ciao, bellas! Allegra here. Just met with a fabulous leather craftsman outside Florence. A true artisan. He makes the most sumptuous braided belts that I am hoping to include in an upcoming collection...

After Emma finished putting the finishing touches on the

blog, she returned to the muslin mash-up of Rylan's dress. "I am in so much trouble with this," she moaned. "It will never fit her."

"No, you're not." Charlie grinned like a girl on her first trip to Tiffany's. "*I* came up with a plan to solve the measurement thing."

"You did? What?" Emma squealed.

"It's a little different. A little weird." He lowered his voice. "Maybe even a little illicit."

That was another favorite Charlie word: *illicit.* He used it as often as he could, usually to describe stuff that wasn't illicit at all.

"Spit it out," Emma insisted.

"Okay. But promise you won't say anything. And remember that desperate times call for desperate measures."

CHAPTER 11

DESPERATE MEASURES

I can't believe I'm seriously about to do this," Emma moaned as she peeked around the corner of the school's narrow hallway the next afternoon. The arched entryway to the high-school half of the girls' locker room was visible about halfway down. "I'm so not the breaking-and-entering type."

"It's not breaking and entering. You have the combo," Charlie reminded her.

She glanced over at him. "Yeah. I still don't want to know how you got that."

"Probably just as well." Charlie smirked.

Emma kept quiet as several high-school football players hurried past. One of them, a no-neck guy with a ruddy face, shot the younger kids a curious look. Emma dropped to one knee and fiddled with the laces of her retro canvas sneakers, hoping she looked natural. Seconds later, the athletes had disappeared out the exit at the far end of the hall.

"What am I going to say if someone catches me on the high-school side of the gym?" Emma asked as she stood.

"People cut through there all the time." Charlie shrugged.

"I guess. But *I* don't." Still, Emma knew he was right. Downtown Day had begun as a much smaller school covering grades six to twelve. It had grown over the years, adding floors and wings to the original brick building. By the time the trustees had decided to split the grades into high school and middle school some years ago, there had been no more space for additions. That was why the two schools shared certain facilities, including the gyms and locker rooms. The latter had been split with only a half-wall separating them.

Due to the layout, entering the middle-school side of the locker room involved a long walk around the perimeter of the gym. Students weren't supposed to take the shortcut through the high-school side, but many still did if they thought none of the faculty was watching.

"I don't know why I listen to your crazy plans, anyway," Emma remarked.

"Because I'm a genius mastermind," Charlie reminded her. "Anyway, who else are you going to listen to? Of course, you could tell Rylan that Allegra had the brilliant idea to make her a caftan instead of a regular dress. My mom practically lives in those things, and I don't think they require any measurements at all. Just a big blob of fabric. Preferably one

gross!

with a hideous floral print that went out of style before anyone we know was born."

"Okay, okay!" Emma giggled and poked him in the arm to shut him up. Then she peered around the corner again. A couple of high-school girls were just coming out of the locker room, so she drew her head back quickly.

"What's the deal with Francesca, anyway?" Charlie continued. "Is she going to be hanging around Laceland all the time, or what?"

"I don't know. Why?"

Charlie lifted one shoulder. "As much as I hate to admit it, she's just kind of…in the way," he said. "I mean, how many times did she knock stuff over yesterday?"

Emma shot him a surprised look. "I thought you were two peas in a pod," she said. "You both cause trouble wherever you go."

"Funny," Charlie said.

"She was fabulous on the phone with Rylan yesterday," Emma reminded him. Francesca had phoned Rylan, checking to be sure she'd received "Allegra's" text, calling the blog to her attention, and then listening to Rylan complain and murmuring sympathetically at the appropriate spots, often in Italian.

As Emma had expected, almost all of Rylan's comments on the dress design involved hating her mother's comments. Rylan wanted to veto them all and put the dress back the way it had been in the first place. Emma felt flattered. She'd *known* that dress would be perfect for Rylan. But she also knew that *Signora* Sinclare was not going to just disappear— or agree with her daughter.

Charlie grunted. "Okay, we need to focus on what we're doing here."

"What *I* am doing here," Emma corrected him. She closed her eyes to try to calm herself, but all she could see was the proud grin on Charlie's face the day before when he'd announced that he'd found out Rylan's gym-locker number and combination.

"You what?" Emma had said. "Why?"

"It's all part of my plan." Charlie had rubbed his hands together. "See, I remembered that Rylan is on the high school's tennis team." He'd paused to grimace. "Actually I didn't so much *remember* as get *reminded*. I overheard these guys drooling over how hot the entire girls' team looked at their match over the weekend wearing their hot new uniforms. A couple of them mentioned Rylan specifically. I'll spare you the details."

"Thanks." Emma had recalled noticing those uniforms, even though she rarely paid much attention to sports. Cute, scarlet-red tennis dresses, each with the team member's name embroidered in white on the collar. She'd been impressed by the tailoring, which was way above the level of most sports outfits she'd ever seen.

"So my plan was born," Charlie had continued. "I realized maybe you don't need to actually measure Rylan herself. You just need the measurements off that tennis dress."

Emma's eyes had widened as she'd realized he was right. "Those dresses are fitted in the same basic places as the dress I'm supposed to be making for Rylan," she'd mused. "If I can get those measurements, I should be able to get my dress close enough to get by at the first fitting…"

"Yo, Secret Agent Rose," Charlie said, breaking Emma out of her fog. He stuck his head around the corner. "Looks like the coast is clear. Ready to go?"

"Not really," Emma said. But she took a deep breath to swallow down her nerves and peeked around the corner again herself. "Come on, let's stand closer to the doorway for a minute and listen. We should be able to hear whether there's anyone still inside."

"You go." Charlie gave her a little shove. "I don't want to get a rep as someone who stands outside girls' locker rooms."

"Coward," Emma muttered. She flipped open her bag and yanked out the tape measure she'd stuck in there that morning, along with a small pad of paper and a pencil. Stuffing it all into the back pockets of faded jeans that she had covered with a patchwork of plaid fabrics, she handed Charlie her bag.

"Good luck," he said, slinging it over his shoulder. "I'll meet you outside at the red bench, okay?"

"Okay."

Emma sidled around the corner. The dank hallway was still empty. She paused for a moment in front of the arched entryway, holding her breath and listening. The old metal lockers in there made a terrible clang whenever they opened or closed, and the low-ceilinged locker room with its chipped 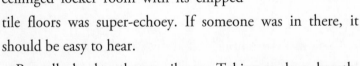 tile floors was super-echoey. If someone was in there, it should be easy to hear.

But all she heard was silence. Taking a deep breath, Emma shot one last glance up and down the hallway and then darted inside.

She was in! The lights were off, but enough daylight

filtered through the high, narrow frosted windows to let her see well enough. Reaching into her pocket, she pulled out the piece of paper where Charlie had scribbled the locker number and combination.

Number forty-two. She looked around and saw that the nearest locker was number six. Great. She was going to have to go in farther.

She crept through the narrow aisles until she finally found the right locker. Then, after another cautious glance around, she started working the combination. Thirty-seven left, fourteen right…Her fingers trembled so badly that she had to start again and again. But finally she heard the lock click.

CLANG! The sound of the locker door swinging open seemed to make as much noise as the subway clattering into the 34th Street station. Emma froze.

For a long moment, nothing happened. Emma started to feel a little light-headed and realized she'd forgotten to breathe. She blew out the breath she'd been holding and sucked in clammier, sweat-scented air. Yuck. The sooner she got out of here, the better.

The tennis dress hung neatly on a hook at the back of the locker. Emma grabbed it and laid it flat on the wooden bench, and then pulled out her tape measure and notebook. Rylan's name, embroidered in snow-white thread, seemed to glow accusingly at her.

It took her only a few seconds to get the measurements she needed. As she'd suspected, they were off more than a bit from the ones Francesca had written down at the meeting. Emma still had no idea how that had happened. As far as she knew, there was no language barrier for numbers. But she wasn't going to worry about it anymore. The important thing was to get done and get out of here.

Tucking the notebook with the new measurements safely back into her pocket, Emma picked up the dress. Despite her nervousness, she couldn't help admiring the way it draped. She held it up against her own body, double-checking the placement of the seams one last time. She definitely didn't want to have to do this again.

"Hey, what are you doing?"

Emma spun around so fast she could literally feel her heart sink to her belly. "Ivana!" she gasped.

Ivana stood at the end of the aisle, hands on hips. "Oh, man, too weird," she exclaimed, taking a step closer. "I was wondering where you were going. Is that Rylan's tennis dress? Why are you clutching it like some crazed stalker?"

Emma gulped. She was so busted. For a second, she was ready to confess everything.

What would Allegra do? Or better yet, what would Charlie do?

That was easy. He'd come up with a cover story on the fly.

Doing her best to channel him, Emma cleared her throat. "Oh, Ivana," she said, trying to sound bored. "You startled me." She quickly turned to hang the tennis dress back in Rylan's locker, giving herself an extra few seconds to think.

When she slammed it shut and turned around, Ivana remained staring at her, arms crossed. "Well?" she demanded.

"Rylan gave me permission to go into her locker to check the dress." Emma grabbed the tape measure, which she'd left on the bench. "See, Allegra wanted me to measure the armscye to make sure that we won't need to edge-stitch the darts in the interfacing."

Okay, so that didn't make a whole lot of sense. But it sounded impressive to toss around all those technical terms, and Emma was counting on that being enough. As far as she knew, Ivana didn't know squat about sewing.

Ivana narrowed her eyes. "Really," she drawled. "That sounds kind of weird to me. Maybe I'd better tell Rylan what I just saw."

"Go ahead," Emma blurted out, suddenly sick of cowing

before Mighty Ivana and her Overwhelming Ego. "Rylan won't care. How do you think I got her locker number if she didn't give it to me? Besides that, what makes you think she'd even listen…to you?"

Ivana's mouth dropped open.

"Fine!" Ivana snapped. "Whatever. I'm going over to Holly's later. Maybe I'll just check it out with Holly's sister—just in case."

Emma couldn't help blanching. If Ivana did that, Emma would be truly busted.

Ivana smirked. She obviously saw she'd struck a nerve.

"Feel free," Emma said as calmly as she could.

"Fine," Ivana said again. "I will." Then she flounced off in triumph toward the middle-school side of the locker room, turning only to add, "Oh, and I'll tell Holls you said hi."

CHAPTER 12

FITS AND STARTS

"Well?" Charlie said, flopping back against the locker next to Emma's the next afternoon. "Anything?"

"Not yet." Emma spun her lock and yanked open her locker, tossing her biology textbook inside. "And it's driving me crazy. I've been waiting for the other Manolo to drop all day."

The final bell had just rung. So far, nobody had said anything to Emma about stalking Rylan. But that hadn't stopped Emma from feeling tense all day.

"So maybe it's going to be okay. Maybe Ivana chickened out and didn't talk to Jennifer," Charlie said.

"Doubtful. She's been smirking at me every chance she gets." Emma shook her head. "Maybe it's Jennifer who hasn't told Rylan yet."

"Or maybe Jennifer forgot about it three seconds after Ivana told her," Charlie countered. "She's kind of a space cadet. No offense to Holly. She obviously got the brains in that family."

Emma didn't dare to be that hopeful just yet. "I wouldn't know. Holly's still avoiding me," she said. "If I could just get her alone, I could make things right."

"Where's she now?"

"No idea," Emma admitted. "Probably with Ivana. Anyway, I need to finish the muslin for Rylan's fitting today. You coming?"

"I can't," Charlie said.

"So meet me at Paige's office later?" Emma closed her locker.

"Nope," Charlie said. "I can't go. I need to see my grandmother. I have no choice. You don't mess with my grandmother."

"Wait." Emma whirled to face him "What are talking about? Grandmother? *Now?*" She gulped. She'd never done anything Allegra without Charlie by her side. "You *can't* send me in there alone."

"You're not alone. You've got Paige…and Francesca," Charlie said. "Look, it'll be fine. You know what to do."

"You think so? *Really?*"

StylePaige
Sweet Heart Appeal

Dear Style Gazers,

Over here at *Madison*, we're counting the days (14!) until the pop-up shop goes live. And we can't wait to share the love!

I've been getting updates from the designers and let me tell you...their delicious new pieces are oh-so-sweet— you are going to Eat Them Up!

C. Leveille is working on a daring double-denim, mad-for-plaid collection.

Allegra Biscotti reports that she is putting final touches on her Return to Childhood collection while in Europe. So jealous. Craving a European vacay—aren't you?

Mario Guo is all about leather-rocker reimagined. I'm itchin' for a wardrobe remix!

Dear readers, I think I'm in love.

Fashionably yours,
Paige Young

"They're here," ponytail-girl called through the intercom on Paige's desk.

Paige punched a button. "Send them in," she ordered.

Emma and Francesca stood stiffly in front of the window opposite the closed office door. I feel like we're waiting for the firing squad, Emma thought. She wondered if Paige had ever felt that way, too. She doubted it. Paige always seemed to be in charge and have everything under control.

The door swung open, admitting Rylan and her mother. Today Mrs. Sinclare was outfitted in a winter-white Yves St. Laurent suit, though she'd ruined its simple elegance with way too much fussy gold jewelry.

"Good afternoon, everyone," Mrs. Sinclare said, her small eyes darting around the room. "Where's Allegra?"

"Oh, dear," Paige said, looking truly shocked. "Didn't my assistant manage to reach you? We found out this morning that Ms. Biscotti's flight was delayed. I'm afraid she won't be able to join us today."

"*Again?*" Mrs. Sinclare said sharply. "Are you serious? This is outrageous!"

Emma hardly heard what Paige said next. She was too intent on watching Rylan. Had Ivana managed to get word of the tennis-dress incident to her yet?

But Rylan's gaze barely skimmed her as she looked around the room. She wandered over to pick up the copy of *Madison*'s latest issue lying on one of the small end tables.

Emma relaxed slightly. Okay, so maybe she hadn't heard. Yet.

She turned back in to Mrs. Sinclare, who was still grumbling about Allegra's absence. Francesca stepped forward.

"Allegra, she asked me to pass on her most humble personal apologies for this unfortunate event, *signora*," she said in her lilting accent. "She was so looking forward to meeting you!"

Mrs. Sinclare still looked annoyed. "Well, I guess she liked my suggestions for the dress, eh?"

"Oh, she knew at once that you are a woman of taste." Francesca beamed at her. "Speaking of which, that suit. It is *splendido!*"

"Thank you, Francesca." Mrs. Sinclare was actually smiling now.

Emma breathed out a silent sigh of relief. Go, Francesca!

Paige stepped forward. "Allegra shipped the muslin for the dress by international overnight, so it's all ready for you to try on."

Emma felt awkward. For one thing, she'd never imagined a situation where she'd be in the same room as Rylan Sinclare in her underwear. Plus, Paige had given Emma and Francesca a script of sorts to work from. She'd instructed Francesca to speak to Emma in Italian, just saying anything that came into her head. Emma was supposed to pretend she understood and "translate" for Rylan. That way, she could ask any questions she needed to or give instructions but make it sound as if it was all coming from Allegra.

To her surprise, the plan worked pretty well. Rylan gave them a strange look now and then, but she didn't say much. In fact, she seemed sort of deflated. She just stood there, moving when someone told her to move, lifting her arms or turning as needed.

Meanwhile her mother was practically purring as she and Paige watched Emma and Francesca fiddle with the muslin.

"It's just as I envisioned it," Mrs. Sinclare said with a pleased little smile. "I can't wait to see it in the proper fabric. When will that be?"

"At the next fitting," Emma said, too distracted by trying to tweak the fit to remember the charade of letting Francesca speak first. "I still need to—er, I mean Allegra needs to—" She shot a helpless glance at Francesca.

Luckily Francesca picked up the cue. "Of course, Allegra has been telling us all how excited she is to search out just the right fabric for this special dress, taking advantage of this unplanned trip to Europe to go to some of her contacts there for the finest of materials." She added something in Italian, then glanced at Emma.

"She says she hopes to have the dress ready in the real fabric by the next fitting," she told Mrs. Sinclare.

"Good, good." Mrs. Sinclare was staring at the muslin.

"Now, I love the way this is looking so far. Much classier. But I wonder if it wouldn't look even better with some sort of collar?"

Emma winced. *Would this woman ever stop?*

"Thanks for opening up today, Dad," Emma said as she and her father stepped out of the elevator into the dark hallway leading to Laceland's empty lobby. It always looked abandoned without Marjorie sitting at the front desk. "I hate to make you come to work on a Saturday. It's just that I still have a ton to do, and there are only two weeks before the pop-up opening."

"You're doing me a favor, Cookie. Your mother was going to drag me to one of those antique book fairs." Noah stepped around the desk and started opening file cabinets. "I'll take lint from lace over dust from yellowed books any day! Just promise me we'll stay long enough so there's no chance I have to go to that thing. Deal?"

"Deal." Emma headed down the hall toward her studio. Just as she reached it, her phone vibrated. She fished it out of her pocket. Charlie.

Downstairs. Buzz me up!

"Charlie's here!" she screamed to her dad, her voice echoing off the sixteen-foot ceilings.

"Got it!" Noah pushed the button to release the lock on the front door. "I'll send him back when he gets up."

"Thanks," Emma called back.

She entered her studio and gently removed the baby-doll dress she'd stitched together the previous day from where she left it on her sewing machine and slid it onto a dress form. Flouncy, soft, feminine, sweet. She loved everything about it. The short hemline and the luscious pink, lavender, blue, and yellow swirls.

On the next dress form, she had started to cut apart Holly's dress and stitch in the brown flannel panels. Sewn into the sides of the dress, the brown pieces wound up accentuating the line, almost outlining it, when you looked at it from the front. She loved how the boyish brown flannel played against the girly pink velvet.

Holly would be so thrilled and surprised when she saw it. That is, if she ever talks to me again, Emma thought. But her eye kept wandering over to the muslin pattern on the third dress form. It was totally distracting. Like a fly on a TV screen. Or a pig at a wedding. Or anything that just...Did. Not. Belong.

"Which of these things is not like the other?" she muttered, as she glanced from the colorful, stylish pop-up outfits to the blah muslin piece that now had a collar, to boot.

"Huh?" Charlie said as he wandered in. "Hey, this is pretty cool," he said, reaching out and touching the beginnings of the princess dress. Emma had begun working on the layers for the skirt, moving them around so she could experiment with which colors played off the best against the others. Should she do pomegranate on top, then burnt orange, then lime? Or should the lime go on top? Or in the middle?

"Which order do you like for the tiers?" she asked Charlie, moving them around as if shuffling cards.

"I can't decide," said Charlie. "It would be cool if you could mix it up. They all look good."

Emma gasped. "Charlie, you're a genius!" she cried.

He looked surprised. "Yeah, I know. We've discussed this before. Remember?" he said.

She grinned. "Funny. No, listen, what you said just gave me a brainstorm."

"Really? What?"

Emma was already dashing across the studio to the battered metal box where she kept zippers, elastic, ribbon, and anything else that was too big to fit into the tins on the worktable. She dug into it and pulled out a roll of Velcro. She would make the tiered dress in a way so that whoever wore it could move the two bottom tiers around. They could even wear just one or two tiers instead of all three if they wanted a shorter look. Each tier just needed some Velcro at the bottom. Just like the party dress with the sash that could be worn lots of different ways, this one could, too!

move layers.

CHAPTER 13

MISMATCHED

So no Allegra?"

"Yes. I'm very sorry," Paige said smoothly. "It's just that—"

Mrs. Sinclare waved her hand dismissively. "Oh, I know. Ms. Biscotti sent a note explaining her absence to my apartment yesterday with lovely flowers and delicious biscotti from Italy. I was dismayed and very concerned, of course, that she has to miss yet another fitting." Mrs. Sinclare sounded oddly resigned to never seeing the phantom designer in person.

Emma shot Paige a relieved look. She could hardly believe their ruse was still working. She and Charlie had been updating the Allegra blog every day or two, adding new yet vague references to various fashion emergencies. Francesca had sent the goodies to Mrs. Sinclare. Emma had also sent another text from Allegra to Rylan, letting her know she'd received her notes and was working them into her latest design.

Rylan stood impatiently next to her mother, while Francesca launched into an Italian-peppered description of all the important things the designer was doing in Europe.

Emma held her breath, hoping Francesca wouldn't contradict anything she'd written on the blog. Luckily, Francesca seemed to have memorized it, though she did embellish a little, adding a glamorous party involving the members of several European royal families, which seemed to impress Mrs. Sinclare.

"With all that travel, I hope she managed to get the dress done," Mrs. Sinclare said, glancing at the garment bag hanging on the hook on the back of the office door.

"*Si*, of course she did indeed! She would not neglect such an important project, *signora*," Francesca assured her earnestly. "The FedEx company, they have been busy rushing your daughter's lovely dress back and forth across the Atlantic to have it ready in time."

"Hmm." Mrs. Sinclare looked rather pleased by that. "All right then, let's see it."

"Good idea." Paige walked over to the garment bag.

Emma had spent the past couple of days working on the dress. It wasn't anything like the first one she'd designed, but she'd ended up liking it. A lot, actually. She had been able to salvage enough of the gracious lines of the original while giving in to Mrs. Sinclare's sleeve and neckline. She'd even stitched a tiny, elegant, stand-up collar that, in a way, restored more of the original neckline. She had given Mrs. Sinclare everything she wanted—well, that is, if the iridescent turquoise could pass for napkin-colored, *plus* the sash that she didn't want.

It wasn't the original black-and-sapphire, sleek, sleeveless dress that would be hanging in the pop-up shop. But it was pretty. It was more than pretty. And Emma was proud of herself for doing what Mrs. Sinclare wanted *and* what Rylan wanted.

She had worked up until the very last minute that afternoon and hadn't been able to find a taxi for the longest time, rushing in just seconds before the Sinclares did, so neither Paige nor Francesca had seen the new and improved dress.

Emma held her breath, watching Paige unzip the garment bag and pull out the dress. Paige raised an eyebrow in surprise.

What was that? Emma wondered. Does she like it?

"That's insane!" Rylan's eyes lit up. "I didn't think anyone could fix that ugly dress. But Allegra so pulled it off! I love it!"

Emma couldn't hold back her grin. Score!

Mrs. Sinclare circled the dress. She rubbed the fabric between her fingers. And then she spoke. "Well, *I* don't love it."

Emma's grin faded. *Thud.*

"What are you talking about?" Rylan shot her mother an irritated look. "It's gorgeous, and it's got *your* color. I'll match the tables."

Mrs. Sinclare shook her head, grabbing the dress and shaking it at Paige. "I thought I told you I despised the sash."

"Are you kidding me?" Rylan grabbed her own head with both hands. "How can you say that? It's the sash that makes it super-sophisticated instead of boring!"

Emma caught herself starting to nod. Rylan got it! Maybe she wasn't the shallow shopaholic Emma had always taken her for. Maybe she did have more individuality than Ivana and her follower friends would ever have.

Francesca started to show Mrs. Sinclare all of the different ways the sash could be wrapped, just as Emma had instructed her. "See, it's so chic," she purred.

"Buttons will make it less boring. And maybe Allegra can throw in a ruffle."

"A ruffle, Mom? You can't be serious!"

Mrs. Sinclare pushed the dress away, scowling at her daughter and everyone else in the room like a caged animal. "Drop the attitude," she hissed at Rylan. "Pronto."

"What attitude?" Rylan's eyes flashed. "You mean the attitude that I want to wear a dress that I actually like at my own Sweet Sixteen? Or the one that my mother doesn't consider me in any decision she makes?"

"We are *not* having this conversation in front of people,"

Mrs. Sinclare warned through gritted teeth. Grabbing her daughter by the arm, she dragged her toward the door. "Pardon us," she called, her voice lilting with false happiness. "We'll be back in a moment."

She steered Rylan through the office door and shut it firmly behind her.

"*Mama mia!*" Francesca murmured.

Paige spun toward Emma. "Are you for real?" she exclaimed. "How could you make major changes like that without at least checking in with me? I thought you understood—"

"No!" Emma burst out, feeling completely confused and emotional and overwhelmed by what had just happened. All she'd wanted to do was make a nice dress that would make everyone happy. How was she supposed to predict that Mrs. Sinclare would react that way?

If she had to stand there and listen to Paige scold her right now, Emma was afraid she might break down completely. And she definitely didn't want to do that in front of Paige. "I *don't* understand! That's the whole problem, okay? Excuse me, I—I need to get out of here for a second."

She rushed out of the office. There was nobody in view in the hallway outside. It was completely empty except for a rack of clothes that someone had left standing askew halfway to the lobby. Emma just stood there for a second, unsure where to go. All she needed was a few minutes alone to figure out what had gone so horribly wrong.

Remembering that she'd noticed a ladies' lounge farther down the hall on a previous visit, she headed that way. Her hand was on the door-knob when she heard raised voices inside and realized this must be where Rylan and her mother had gone.

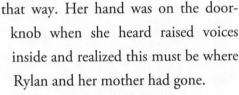

She almost turned and ran the other way. But she hesitated, a little curious in spite of everything.

"…and I don't know where your father and I went wrong with you, Rylan!" Mrs. Sinclare was saying roughly.

"I try to make you proud of me!" Rylan protested, her voice sounding ragged around the edges. "I just—"

"Don't interrupt me when I'm talking to you!" Mrs. Sinclare snapped. "You just don't appreciate what we do for you. You need to grow up and realize you can't have every-thing exactly as you want all the time."

"Why not?" Rylan shouted. "You do!"

"How dare you?" her mother thundered.

Emma winced as Mrs. Sinclare started ranting again. Her

voice was so loud, even through the closed restroom door, that it was difficult to hear much else. But Emma picked up another, softer sound beneath it. Was Rylan crying?

Wow. So the Queen of Mean of Downtown Day actually had real, honest-to-goodness feelings. Who knew?

After another minute or two of Mrs. Sinclare's tirade, Emma was ready to creep off, feeling guilty about listening. But finally Mrs. Sinclare's tone changed.

"Stop that crying, Rylan," she said, sounding more confused than angry all of a sudden. "I don't know why you're so upset about this, anyway. It's just too bad that silly maid ruined your first dress. That one was perfect. None of this messing around with world-traveling designers and such."

"Yeah," Rylan said with a loud sniffle. "Too bad."

"Pull yourself together," her mother ordered. "In the meantime, I'll go speak to Francesca about ripping the ribbons off the dress." She sighed loudly. "I just hope there's not some kind of language barrier holding us back here…"

Emma barely had time to jump behind the abandoned rack of clothes in the hallway before the restroom door flew open and Mrs. Sinclare marched out. The woman headed for Paige's office, looking neither left nor right. A second later she disappeared inside.

Whew. Emma stepped out of her hiding place. She definitely wanted to make herself scarce before Rylan emerged.

"Hold it right there," Rylan commanded. Her tears were already gone.

Emma froze.

Uh-oh. Too late.

CHAPTER 14

IN(VITE) WITH THE IN CROWD

Get in here," Rylan ordered.

When Emma didn't move, the older girl grabbed her by the wrist and gave her a rough yank. That finally started Emma's feet working. She stumbled forward, caught herself, and then meekly followed Rylan through the restroom door.

For a second, she found herself totally distracted by her first glimpse of the ladies' lounge, which like everything else at *Madison* was gorgeous and elegantly appointed. Cool marble counters held big marble bowls for sinks. Copper faucets gleamed under copper-framed mirrors. It looked more like a luxury hotel room than the home of the local toilet.

"What did you just hear?" Rylan asked.

"Um, nothing?" Emma replied. "I mean…what do you mean?"

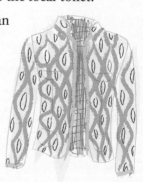

Rylan frowned. "Come on, I know you were listening," she said. "So just tell me. Are you going to rat me out about the first dress? I mean, your mom's smart so you probably are, too. I'm sure you've probably put two and two together by now."

Emma's eyes widened. "Wait," she blurted out as her mind flashed back to that Saturday afternoon at Holly's place. "You mean…you mean *you* ruined your original party dress?"

"A real genius," Rylan said sarcastically. "I know you heard us talking about it that day at Jen's."

Emma was a little surprised. She hadn't even been sure Rylan had noticed she was the same girl from that day at Holly's. But that wasn't really the point right now.

"So what happened?" she asked tentatively, more than a little fearful of Rylan's stormy expression but too curious not to ask.

Rylan looked annoyed. "Oh, just the usual," she said. "Mother shipped in a dress from some designer out in L.A. that her airheaded friend told her about and insisted I had to wear it to my party. But of course it was horrible. Something my grandmother would wear to church. No way was I going to let anyone at school see me in something like that." Her eyes narrowed as she peered at Emma.

"Then I saw those spring dresses Allegra Biscotti designed on Paige's blog, and they're hot. I don't want to dress like my mother. But I don't want to dress like a kid either. I knew Allegra could design the perfect dress." She shrugged. "So I destroyed the other dress by tossing it in the dryer with a pair of jeans with a bright red lipstick in the pocket."

"Wow," Emma said, trying to imagine doing anything like that. But she shook her head. She couldn't. She might take the ugly dress apart and rebuild it as something else, but she'd never have the guts to do something so extreme.

"Yeah," Rylan said. "So when Mother found out, she hit the roof. Luckily I managed to blame it on one of the maids." She smirked. "I talked Mother into trying Allegra instead of going back to Mr. Boring L.A. Designer, and the rest was history." She bit her lip. "But now, thanks to Mommy Dearest and some color-blind party planner, I'm still going to be stuck looking horrible."

"What happened to the maid?" Emma asked.

"Fired," Rylan replied.

Emma's first reaction was to feel sorry for the maid. But Rylan looked so wrecked that Emma felt a pang of sympathy for her, too. Emma's mother might be kind of bossy and unreasonable sometimes, not to mention obsessed with academics and pretty much nothing else in life. But Emma wanted to rush right home, hug her, and promise to take every advanced class that Downtown Day offered just out of sheer gratitude that she hadn't been born Mrs. Sinclare's daughter instead.

An enormous mirror framed in hammered copper covered most of one wall of the lounge, and Rylan wandered over and stared into it. "I can't believe Mother is ruining this for me," she said.

Emma kept quiet. She had the distinct feeling that Rylan was talking to herself more than to her. In fact, she wasn't sure the other girl remembered she was still there. Invisible Emma strikes again.

"That first dress Allegra sketched would've been epic," Rylan went on into the mirror. "The lines were great. Really flattering while still looking totally cutting edge. And I love all of the fabrics she sent, too." She sighed. "I so would've loved to wear *that* dress. Talk about making an entrance!"

Yeah. Rylan was all about making a splash everywhere she went—being noticed, being first with the newest, hippest thing.

But Emma was stuck on the first part of what Rylan had just said. She couldn't help remembering the way Rylan had reacted to the redesigned dress just now. And to the original design, for that matter. That hadn't been all about the name on the label.

"I'm glad you liked it," she blurted out. "I really

thought it would be perfect for…" Her voice trailed off as Emma suddenly remembered where she was. *Who* she was. And who she *wasn't*, at least as far as Rylan knew.

She gulped. As tempting as it was, she couldn't let Rylan know exactly how well she understood. "I mean, I think Allegra really got what you wanted," she said lamely. "I know Francesca and I both told her all about you so she'd understand who she was designing for. Sounds like it worked."

"Yeah, I guess. Of course it might have worked better if she'd ever bothered to show up for these fittings." Rylan's voice and expression were bitter. "Maybe if she'd been here, Mother couldn't have steamrolled her like she did the rest of you." Then she glanced into the mirror again. "Then again, maybe it wouldn't have mattered. She thinks she knows what's best for everyone, and she won't be happy until she turns me into a clone of my three perfect older sisters."

"Oh." Emma was surprised. "I didn't even know you had sisters. Did they go to Downtown Day?"

"Of course. And everyone there always expects me to be just as perfect and obedient as they were. They're all like Mother's little robots." Suddenly seeming to remember who she was talking to, Rylan turned to face Emma. "So I suppose it's going to be all over school by tomorrow," she said, her face hard and fierce.

"Um, what?" Emma said uncertainly.

Rylan glared at her. "You know. This. Today. How Rylan Sinclare's mommy made her cry. About how she doesn't even get to pick out what she's going to wear to her own party. All the rest of this garbage." She smirked humorlessly. "You could make your social life at Downtown Day with a juicy little nugget like that."

"Of course not!" Emma shook her head. "I'm not going to tell anyone anything. I can keep a secret."

If Rylan only knew how true that was, she wouldn't be so worried.

Rylan narrowed her eyes, sizing up Emma's expression. Finally she relaxed, shrugging off the mean veneer like a too-warm coat.

"I hope you're for real," she said, sounding kind of tired.

Emma chanced a small, tentative smile.

Rylan's smile in return was brief but looked sincere. Then she glanced at the door.

As they stepped back into Paige's office, Emma quickly surveyed the scene. Paige stood behind her desk, idly flipping through possible photos for an upcoming issue. Francesca was charming Mrs. Sinclare over near the windows. Charlie was slumped in one of the guest chairs, clearly wishing he were anywhere else. He shot Emma a curious look as she entered, but all she had time to do was shrug before Rylan stepped forward.

"Listen, everyone," Rylan said. "I want to apologize for

running out like that. I'm *soooo* sorry to have put all of you through all the hassle of these redesigns and everything."

"It's all right, Rylan," Paige said. "It's just part of the process. We really don't—"

"Wait, I'm not finished," Rylan interrupted. "To make up for the extra work, I want to invite all of you to my Sweet Sixteen party as my special guests." She turned and looked at each of them in turn—Paige, Francesca, Charlie, and then Emma. When Emma met her eye, she was sure she saw an evil twinkle in it. "And feel free to bring a date if you like," Rylan added. "Or two or three of your friends, or whatever. If Allegra gets back to town in time, she should totally come, too."

Mrs. Sinclare took a quick step forward, looking alarmed. "But we've already cut the guest list…" Her voice trailed off and, for the first time since Emma had met her, she seemed less than fully in command of the situation. "I mean, yes, of course," she finished. "You're certainly all welcome if you think you'd be comfortable attending."

"Thank you for the generous invitation, Rylan," Paige said. "Unfortunately, I'll be tied up with a work function that evening, but I'm sure it will be quite a party."

"Oh, it will." Rylan glanced around at the others. "The rest of you will come, though, won't you?" Her gaze stopped on Emma, and she stared at her.

Emma wasn't sure what to say. Most of Downtown Day would kill for an invitation to Rylan Sinclare's Sweet Sixteen. But it wasn't really her kind of scene, to say the least. Plus, the pop-up shop would be open that same weekend, and Emma had assumed she'd be hanging out there every chance she got.

"We're totally there," Charlie piped up. "Wouldn't miss it for the world. Right, Emma?"

"Um, sure," Emma said, shooting him a surprised look. Since when was he Mr. Social Party Boy? She would have thought he'd rather spend an evening watching his mother's worst drama student in some so-far-off-Broadway-it's-actually-in-New-Jersey production of *A Chorus Line* than hanging out with Rylan and her crowd.

"Oh, *sicuramente*, I will be there, too," Francesca gushed. "I cannot wait to attend, *signorina*. It is so sweet of you to make such an invitation!"

"Good. And definitely bring friends. Mother and Daddy are sparing no expense. After all, you only turn sixteen once, right?" Rylan sounded pleased with herself.

"Yes. More's the pity." Mrs. Sinclare's tone was icy. "Now, I have things to do." She turned to Paige. "See to it that

Allegra fixes the dress and gets rid of that ribbon. I *really* don't want to bring my husband into this. He gets…well, let's just avoid that, shall we?" She shot Paige a meaningful look. "We'll see you at the next fitting. Come, Rylan."

She strode out of the office. Rylan hesitated, her eyes locking with Emma's for a brief, curious moment, and then she followed her mother.

"Oh, man," Paige muttered when they were gone. "That was…something."

"I'm really sorry," Emma blurted out, grabbing the criss-cross ribbon dress from Paige and quickly zipping it back into its garment bag. "I thought I was, you know, compromising. I thought this new design was something Rylan and her mom might both like."

Paige sighed and sat down behind her desk. "I know you were," she said. Everything about Paige suddenly slowed down. "And I'm the one who should probably apologize. Sometimes I forget you're really still just a kid. I can't expect you to know all the ins and outs of this industry. And people like *her*."

Emma kept quiet, not sure where this was going. Charlie and Francesca were listening silently as well.

"The main point is," Paige went on, "a designer and a client really need to be a team, working toward the same goal. It's like me and my wedding-dress designer."

175

Emma nodded. She'd first met Paige when she'd come to Laceland to look at materials for the dress she was having made for her upcoming wedding. Her designer had been there, too, and had spent a lot of time reassuring Paige that the dress would be perfect. Definitely a team player.

"Okay, I hear that," Emma said. "But this is different, right? First off, you have great style. I know you keep saying that Mrs. Sinclare is the client because she's paying the bill. But Rylan's the one who has to wear the dress. What am I supposed to do if the two of *them* aren't a team?"

"I'll tell you what you're supposed to do," Paige said, revving back into fashion-executive mode. "You make Mrs. Sinclare happy. Lose the sash. Add some buttons and a ruffle. And let her deal with her daughter. It has to be that way this time."

Emma could tell that Paige thought this was all really simple. But Emma was conflicted. Could she really go along with what Paige was saying when she really wanted to stick with the dress that Rylan preferred, the one that would make her look and feel amazing on her special day? Wasn't that what fashion was all about? A way to express yourself to the world? To make the wearer feel self-confident and beautiful?

But she knew what Paige would say. What she *had* said.

Emma wondered how she could do that to Rylan.

"Did you hear Ivana and the Bees talking after geometry class about Rylan's party?" Charlie grinned at Emma as the two of them climbed the steps leading out of the 34th Street subway station. "They're so dying for an invite. I really wanted to tell them we scored an exclusive invite. It's killing me."

"*I* still can't believe you actually want to go," Emma countered. "Who are you, and what have you done with Charlie?"

He grinned. "Okay, so the actual party will probably be a joke. Just a bunch of snobs all trying to out-snobbify one another. Total train wreck. But don't you want to watch Ivana's head explode when she finds out we were there? I'm already planning the choice photos I can upload onto Facebook. Now that's going to sting our little Ivana and her Bees when *she* is revealed to be the social outcast."

Emma had to admit it was a slightly delicious thought, though she hadn't had much time to dwell on the actual party. It was hard to believe an entire week had gone by since the fitting. It had passed in a mostly happy blur of cutting, stitching, and draping the pieces for the pop-up collection. The babydoll dress looked happy even hanging on a hanger. She'd moved it off the dress form once she finished it to make room for the other dresses.

Yesterday she had played around with lace samples her father had given her to layer over the tights that would go underneath the babydoll dress as leggings. She thought she'd found the perfect stretchy weave. She just needed to track down the perfect pale-pink tights to go underneath the lace.

The princess dress now hung on the dress form. She attached the first pomegranate-colored tier to the gold top. Adding the Velcro to the moveable burnt orange and lime tiers would mean much less sewing. She still had to tidy up the neckline. The gold knit fabric was tricky to work with, but it fell beautifully and looked gorgeous with the palette of this dress. Totally SoHo princess.

The cobalt and black dress she'd originally designed for Rylan was complete and displayed on another dress form. She had just sewn a tiny brown-flannel collar onto the pink velvet dress. Once she replaced the zipper, that one would be done, as well.

Then she would tackle her *ah-mazing* accessory idea. She'd found an old, clear Lucite purse, filled to the top with buttons, that Grandma Grace had given to her for her ninth birthday. It was a beautiful vintage piece from the 1920s, and Emma loved the sound it made when she snapped the gold closure.

She lined the purse with fabric remnants, giving her a purse that coordinated with each of the very different dresses she had made. With a big square of lollipop silk tucked inside, it was the swingy, hip partner to the babydoll dress. A length of sapphire satin lining made it an exquisite match for the party dress. And any one—or all three—of the princess-tier colors stuffed inside made it look gorgeous with that dress, too! She was almost ready for the grand-opening press party on Friday night.

Then there was Rylan's dress.

Emma wasn't quite so happy about that.

She'd remade it to Mrs. Sinclare's specifications. She'd found tiny, tiny turquoise crystal buttons and run them down the back of the dress. She hadn't really known what to do with the ruffle. She added a tiny ruffle to the end of the sleeves, hoping that would suffice. It was the most ruffle she was willing to give. But without that sash, this dress was something any fourteen-year-old with a sewing machine (and a Grandma Grace and a Marjorie) could have designed, and she knew it.

She kept trying to figure out if there was anything

else she could do to save the design. She needed just one magical idea.

But how could she fix the dress when she wasn't allowed to change the parts that looked the worst?

Sure, she'd had sewing problems before. Plenty of them. She'd made dresses with crooked zippers, jackets with uneven armholes, and pants that had mismatched legs. But she still loved them, imperfections and all, because she believed in her designs.

Emma sighed heavily, realizing she was just going to have to live with sending a dress out into the world that her heart wasn't in. She dreaded seeing Rylan wearing it Saturday night. But according to Charlie, they were going, no matter what.

"Don't get too excited about your new social fabulousness or anything," Emma told him as they reached the top of the steps. "I'm sure Rylan just did it to get back at her mom and make sure the party would be even more expensive than they'd planned by inviting a bunch of extra people. She even texted me to say I could invite all of Allegra's other employees, too."

"Maybe we should do her a favor and just start inviting random people off the street."

Emma didn't say anything. She had almost done just that today. Sort of.

During world history, she'd turned and glimpsed Jackson staring at her as she doodled in the margins of her notebook. She'd pretended not to notice as she tried to process this startling turn of events. For the last three months, *she* had stared at *him* in class. She'd tried desperately to fight the urge but failed daily, her eyes drawn almost magnetically to him.

And now that he was an item with Lexie, the boy of her dreams was looking at *her?* What sense did that make? She momentarily summoned the courage to ask him to the party but immediately chickened out.

Besides, she told herself, there was Lexie.

"It's freezing out here." Charlie pulled his fuzzy-lined motorcycle jacket closed as the cold winter air whipped across 37th Street from the Hudson River. "Let's hurry. Laceland awaits."

"Hold on. I need to make a stop at Allure first," Emma told him. "I need to pick up a little pink nylon for the leggings."

"Do I have to come?" Charlie wrinkled his nose. "Fabric stores make me sleepy. All that material begs to be wrapped around me like a blanket."

"How would you know? You've never even been in one!" Emma laughed. "Go ahead. I'll meet you at Laceland in a few."

Emma turned and hurried the few blocks to the fabric store.

She looked for Nidhi when she got inside but didn't see her. It must be her day off, Emma realized. Probably just as well. This way, she could get what she needed and get out, back to the safety of Laceland, where everybody knew her secrets and she didn't have to sneak around or lie.

A few minutes later, she was in the creaky, wheezing elevator on her way up to Laceland. She peeked into the Allure bag and smiled at the fabric nestled there, like a pretty tropical flower just waiting to bloom. She was excited to finish up the leggings, go over all of her seams, and tie up her pop-up collection.

"Clear the way, everyone!" she sang out cheerfully as she pushed open the heavy door to Laceland, swinging her Allure bag. "Allegra Biscotti is here, and she has work to do!"

The grin froze on her face.

Standing in front of Marjorie's desk, staring at her, was... Holly.

CHAPTER 15

TRUTH AND CONSEQUENCES

Holly!" Emma blurted out, her mind racing. How much had Holly heard?

She shot a desperate look around the lobby area. Marjorie sat in her chair, her face frozen in an expression of dismay. Francesca and Charlie stood alongside the desk, staring at Emma in shock.

Then there was Holly. She waited silently, wrapped in her favorite puffy, white down jacket and glaring at her.

"Um—hi!" Emma stammered. "I was just saying that I need to take this fabric back so Allegra can…"

She trailed off as she spotted Charlie shaking his head at her. "Give it up," he said. "She already knows the truth. Or at least way too much of it. Thanks to you-know-who."

He tilted his head toward Francesca, who clasped her hands and leaped forward. Even in the midst of what was happening, Emma couldn't help admiring Francesca's perfectly tailored chocolate wool pantsuit, peach silk tank, and high-heeled Mary Janes.

"I'm so sorry, Emmita!" Francesca cried. "When this *ragazza bella* said she was your best friend, I naturally assumed—"

"*Former* best friend," Holly put in, her voice as cold and sharp as the icicles hanging over the doorway downstairs.

Francesca was still talking, not seeming to hear her. "How was I to know she was not part of the secret?" she exclaimed sorrowfully.

"It's not your fault," Holly said to Francesca. "Any normal person would assume that best friends tell each other everything. I mean, that's what *I* always assumed, until now."

"Get over yourself, Holly," Charlie put in with a frown. "Anyway, Francesca shouldn't have—"

"I didn't mean to—"

"It's not like I hadn't already figured it out before she—"

All three of them started talking at once. Only Emma and Marjorie remained silent. Marjorie's head moved back and forth from speaker to speaker as if she were watching a particularly fast-paced tennis match.

As she listened, Emma quickly caught on to the gist of what had happened. Holly had checked out the Allegra Biscotti website and realized that a lot of things on it looked oddly familiar. Some of the dresses. The style of sketching. And especially that shot of the inspiration wall. At first she hadn't quite understood what she was seeing.

But Holly was clever—more so than people actually gave her credit for. She'd figured out what had to be happening here, as crazy as it seemed. As soon as she did, she'd rushed over to Laceland to confront Emma. When she'd entered, Francesca had been covering the front desk while Marjorie was powdering her nose in the ladies' room, and when Holly had introduced herself as Emma's best friend, Francesca had assumed she knew the truth about Allegra.

"By the time I realized my terrible mistake, it was too late!" Francesca cried, waving her hand so her oversized men's watch jingled.

"Don't beat yourself up," Holly told her. She rolled her eyes in Charlie's direction. "Having Mr. Smooth rush out and start babbling to try to cover for you didn't exactly help. Anyway, I'd already figured it out before I got here."

Emma could see the hurt and confusion radiating from Holly's eyes. And no wonder. Why had she allowed Paige to bully her into keeping something so important from her best friend?

But all that was over. Holly knew now. Paige could rant and complain all day, but she couldn't change that.

"Excuse us," she said, grabbing Holly's hand. "We need to talk. Privately."

"There's nothing to talk about." Holly tried to yank her hand away, but Emma held on. She knew they had to hash this out here and now, or it really could mean the end of their friendship.

"Come on," she said, giving Holly a tug to pull her toward the hallway. "Please?"

Holly hesitated, then shrugged and followed Emma into the studio.

"Wow," Holly said, glancing around. "You've really added a lot of stuff to this place since the last time I was here."

Emma didn't bother to point out that Holly hadn't been there for a *really* long time. This year, sitting around a lace warehouse watching Emma sew didn't provide the same excitement as hanging out with Ivana and her clique.

But that wasn't the point either. At least not right now.

"I'm really sorry, Holls," Emma said. "I never meant to keep secrets from you."

"Then why did you?" Holly challenged, crossing her arms.

"I'm not sure. It just sort of happened, and then things got out of control, and well…" Emma took a deep breath. "Look, maybe I should just tell you everything and how it happened and that might help you understand, okay?"

"Whatever." Holly leaned back against one of Emma's work stools, waiting.

"Okay. It all started the day Paige Young came to Laceland…" Emma continued the story from there, pouring out all those early details. Paige seeing some dresses in her studio and demanding to know who'd designed them. Emma making up the name "Allegra Biscotti" on the spot, as Charlie watched in amusement.

"Then things started to get complicated," Emma continued. "Paige featured the dresses—and Allegra Biscotti—on her blog," she said. "It was really cool, and trust me, I was *dying* to tell you about it. But every time I tried, someone would interrupt. Mostly Ivana."

She gave Holly a sidelong glance. Holly had perched on one of the stools by now and had grabbed a scrap of fabric, which she was twisting between her fingers as she listened. She looked perplexed. "But Ivana's not *always* around," she protested.

"It sure seems like it." Emma tried not to sound bitter, but she wasn't sure she'd succeeded. "Anyway, like I said, I tried to tell you a few times. But then before I could, Paige found out that Allegra was really fourteen-year-old me and totally freaked out. She made me swear not to tell anyone else."

"And a promise to some bossy fashion editor you just met is more important to you than *me?*" Holly asked with a frown.

"No, of course not," Emma said. "But I knew it was totally important to keep Allegra Biscotti's true identity a secret, or else my fashion career would be finished before it had barely gotten started. And, well…" She hesitated, not quite sure how to say the next part since it was probably going to make Holly mad. But she was trying to be honest here, right? "Um, I wasn't sure you'd, you know, be able to keep such a huge secret."

Holly looked hurt again. "Are you kidding me?" she exclaimed. "Since when can't you trust me, Em?"

"Since you started telling Ivana everything," Emma said.

"I do not!"

"Really? You showed her my sketch of Jackson that time." Emma's cheeks still felt hot. During a shopping trip to Bloomingdale's with Ivana and the Bees, she'd showed Holly some drawings she'd made of Jackson in her sketchbook. Holly had turned right around and told Ivana and the others about them.

"You mean that time at Bloomie's?" Holly said. "That was ages ago."

"I know. And I know you were trying to be nice, like telling them I was a good artist and stuff," Emma said. "But I really didn't want them to see it, and you didn't even ask, and so I had to wonder…"

"Oh, give it up, Em. I knew you were embarrassed about that, but I already told you I was sorry," Holly said. "Anyway, I might have messed up there, you're totally right. But in my defense, I had no idea those sketches were supposed to be some big secret. Plus, I've been keeping your other secret for like weeks now, and Ivana doesn't even know."

Emma was still focused on that embarrassing moment at Bloomingdale's. It took her a second to take in what Holly had just said.

"Huh?" she said. "What other secret? You mean about me being Allegra?"

"No, I'm talking about the other thing," Emma replied.

"What other thing?"

"The locker-room thing." Holly shrugged. "Ivana came over one day and seemed, like, really disappointed that Jen wasn't home. Which is weird because Jen hardly ever even talks to Ivana when she's over."

"Okay," Emma agreed.

"Anyway, when I asked Ivana what was up with that, she told me about catching you going into Rylan Sinclare's gym locker," Holly went on. "She seemed pretty sure you were up to something weird. She had all these crazy stalker ideas about you. It didn't really sound like it to me, especially since I knew by then that you were Allegra Biscotti's intern. Or whatever."

"Right," Emma said.

"Anyway, Ivana was really worked up about it. She made me promise to tell Jen all about it as soon as I saw her and to tell her to be sure to let Rylan know."

Emma bit her lip. With everything else that had been going on since then, she'd almost forgotten about the tennis-dress incident. So Ivana really *had* tried to put her evil plan into action!

"I can't believe she was really going to rat me out," she muttered. "Typical."

"Don't worry. I didn't breathe a word to Jen," Holly assured her.

"Thanks," Emma said. "But what about Ivana? Wasn't she mad?"

"Oh, she totally thinks I told her." Holly's mouth twitched. "Like, every day after that she'd come in and be all, did Jen tell Rylan yet? Did she tell Rylan yet?"

Emma almost smiled. Holly did a pretty good Ivana impression. "What do you say?"

"I just kept playing innocent." The tiniest of giggles escaped from Holly's lips. "It took her like a week to get over it. I guess she thinks either Jen forgot to tell Rylan, or she did tell her and Rylan didn't care."

"Wow," Emma said, not quite sure how to feel. Talk about a close call! What would Rylan have done if she'd found out about Emma breaking into her gym locker? Never mind Allegra Biscotti. Emma would have had to move to Timbuktu or Antarctica or somewhere just to avoid dying of embarrassment.

"Yeah," Holly said. "Ever since then, Ivana just sort of growls any time your name comes up."

Emma could imagine it perfectly. The whole situation was so ridiculous that she couldn't help giggling, the laughter bubbling up out of her. Despite still looking kind of upset, Holly was smiling a little now, too.

"What's so funny?" she said.

"Nothing," Emma said. "Sorry. It's just...I can so picture it. Ivana standing there looking all cool and perfect, with her face all twisted up like a wet cat while she wonders why the heck Rylan isn't tearing my head off right that second."

Holly looked surprised, but then she shrugged. "Yeah," she admitted. "That kind of sounds like Ivana. She usually gets what she wants, so whenever she doesn't, she kind of goes a little nutso." This time she was the one who laughed. Within seconds, both of them were laughing so hard they couldn't stop.

"Whew!" Holly said finally, leaning against a stool and clutching her stomach. "That felt good."

"Yeah. But listen, I still need to tell you the rest," Emma said. "I want you to know everything. Like you should have from the start. But—"

"But what?"

"I hate to have to ask you this, Holls, but I have to," Emma said. "You won't tell anyone about Allegra Biscotti and me, will you?"

"You can trust me," Holly promised. "For real."

"So you won't tell Ivana or Lexie or *any*one?"

"I *said* I wouldn't. No one. Pinkie swear." Holly held out her pinkie finger the way they used to make a promise when they were young.

Emma linked her pinkie with Holly's and smiled.

"Okay," Holly said. "I am kind of curious how you ended

up getting hired to make Rylan's Sweet Sixteen dress. And how you kept her from noticing that Allegra Biscotti is really some eighth-grader from her own school. I mean, I know important social goddesses like her don't pay much attention to us little people, but still…"

Emma grinned. "Yeah, that was kind of a tricky one," she said. "You know the Italian girl out front? Well, she was interning at Paige's office…" She was off and running, telling Holly the rest of the story.

As she listened, Holly grabbed a tissue from the box on the corner of the worktable, dabbing at her eyes, which were damp from laughing until she cried. She stood to drop the used tissue in the wastebasket and stared wide-eyed at the inspiration wall.

"Hey," she said, interrupting Emma's explanation about the pop-up shop collection. "What's this?"

Emma followed Holly's gaze to the photo of the two of them in the park as little girls. "Remember that?" Emma said. "It was that day in the park. The one we were talking about that time at your place after we found your old dress."

"Wow." Holly leaned over the desk for a closer look. "Look at how adorable we were back then! We've totally got matching lollipop stains all over our faces."

"I know." Emma smiled at her, really glad that they were back to normal again. "I turned your old pink dress into one of the pieces for the pop-up shop, and I actually made a dress inspired by the lollipops, too. Even bought this gorgeous shimmering, swirly fabric that reminded me of the colors."

"Really? Which one is it?" Holly whirled around as Emma pulled the baby-doll dress off the rack with one hand and the redesigned pink velvet with her other hand. "I was going to give this one to you after the shop closed," she told Holly, waving the pink velvet dress at her.

"Those are awesome, Emma! Is that really for me?"

Emma nodded. "I wish I could let you wear it now, but the pop-up shop is open all weekend for store buyers and magazine writers and I don't know who else."

"No biggie," Holly said. "It's not like I have any parties to go to."

"Well," Emma began with a sly smile. "You might. If you happen to be free this Saturday night, that is."

CHAPTER 16

FINISHING TOUCHES

A little to the left," Emma mumbled through a mouthful of pins.

"Like this?" Holly turned slightly to one side, holding her arms out away from the sides of the babydoll dress she wore. She was the perfect sample size, which meant she fit into all the outfits Emma had made for the shop. Being able to see exactly how the clothes moved on a real person helped Emma make some crucial adjustments.

"Perfect." Emma stuck a few more pins in the hem, then spit the rest into her palm and tossed them onto her worktable. "I have to sew it up and press it, and this one will be ready to go, too."

Charlie watched from his perch on a chair in the corner, his feet up on the edge of the worktable. "Yeah, and with a whole thirty seconds to spare," he drawled.

"Don't exaggerate." Holly shot him

a chiding look as she slipped out of the dress. "Marjorie said the messenger from *Madison* won't be here until four thirty, and it's barely four fifteen!"

It was Thursday afternoon. Even though Holly had known about Allegra for a whole three days now, Emma still couldn't get over how good it felt to have *both* her best friends helping her in the final rush to finish everything for the pop-up collection.

Emma flicked on the power switch to her sewing machine, slipped the hem in place, and pressed her foot down on the pedal. She expertly guided the fabric, sewing a straight line of almost invisible stitches. "Charlie," she called over the whir of the motor. "I need the Allegra garment bags. Marjorie should be finished steaming the party dress, so you can pack that one up."

"You got it, boss." Charlie stood and headed toward the rolling rack in the corner of the studio, where Emma had hung the canvas garment bags. Charlie had printed the Allegra Biscotti logo on them as a surprise for her when she'd created her first mini-collection.

"What about me?" Holly asked.

"Can you try to find me some more pink thread?"

"No problem, Em." Holly threw on an oversized button-down oxford shirt, rolled up the sleeves, and hurried over to the worktable to search through the box of sewing-machine thread.

By the time Marjorie bustled back to the studio to say that the messenger was there, Emma, Holly, and Charlie had everything ready to go. Emma let out a sigh of relief and satisfaction as they all watched the guy disappear back into the elevator with a rolling rack full of Allegra Biscotti garment bags.

"My first collection on its way into the fashion world," Emma whispered.

Then the elevator dinged again. Emma saw the dial moving slowly upward. "Uh-oh, did I forget something? It looks like he's coming back."

The doors slid open, and Francesca sang out, "*Ciao, amicos!*"

"The messenger's not with you?" Emma asked nervously.

"No. He stepped off when I stepped on. Your clothes are traveling to *Madison*!" She swung a tiny pastel-colored shopping bag. "I found the most wonderful little Italian bakery on my way here, and I've brought *bocconotti* for everyone for celebration."

"Awesome!" Holly rushed over to peer into the bag. "Ooh, little cream-puff thingies! Yum! You're the best, Francesca. How'd you know I was seriously craving sugar right now?"

Francesca giggled. "I am psycho, no?" she said.

"Psychic!" Holly corrected with a laugh. "You're psychic, you mean."

"Actually, I think she got it right the first time," Charlie muttered.

Emma hid a grin. She could tell it was driving Charlie nuts that Holly and Francesca had hit it off like long-lost tall, slim, fashionable sisters. In fact, Holly was fitting in at Laceland better than Emma ever would have guessed.

"I'd better pack up Rylan's dress," Emma said. "I promised I would messenger it today, too."

"I just hope she's not planning another laundry accident," Holly said as she and Charlie followed Emma down the hall. "Having it in her possession for a full forty-eight hours gives her plenty of time to concoct some horrible end for that poor dress."

Emma nodded. She'd told her friends about Rylan's confession. "I know, right?" she said. "But I doubt she'd pull the same stunt twice. Her mother can't be that clueless. Well, maybe she can, but that would leave Rylan with nothing to wear to the party."

"Yeah. She'd have to show up either in a dress she's worn before or something off the rack." They'd reached the studio by now, and Holly cast a dubious look at the drab dress. "I'm not sure either one of those would be a worse choice.

No offense," she added quickly with an apolo~~g~~
Emma. "I know you did what you could."

"No offense taken." Emma examined the
It looked even more pathetic now that the pop-up pieces
were gone. At least they'd offered a distraction from its
awkward plainness.

"Don't worry, Em. If anyone can pull it off, it's Rylan,"
Holly said. "By Monday, everyone in school will be wearing
this exact same look."

"Ugh, I hope not." Emma shuddered as she pictured Ivana
and her hive prancing down the halls of Downtown Day
wearing identical ugly pea-soup dresses. "With any luck,
Rylan will ban cameras from the party, and nobody will ever
have to know about it."

"Dream on," Charlie said. "Ivana and Lexie will probably
be peeking in the windows." He grinned at Holly. "Tell us
again how apoplectic they were when they heard we were
invited and they're not."

"Apo-what?" Holly wrinkled her nose. "Anyway, be nice,
Charlie. Not everyone gets to be in Allegra Biscotti's entou-
rage. It's not kind to make fun of the less fortunate."

Emma smiled weakly as Charlie laughed. She hadn't quite
gotten around to telling Holly that, according to Rylan, she
was allowed to bring as many guests as she liked. She knew
Holly hadn't turned her back on Ivana and the others. And

199

ma definitely didn't want Ivana at the party. Especially now that she and Holly were tight again.

She wanted Holly to herself, at least for as long as she could have her.

"I thought today was never going to end!" Emma exclaimed as she rushed up to her locker on Friday after school.

Holly popped the pale-pink bubble she'd just blown. "Me too! I swear world history class lasted like forty-two zillion hours. Which is only like a zillion hours more than usual, but still."

Emma yanked open her locker and tossed her books inside. "At least it's over now. Come on, let's find Charlie and get out of here. I'm dying to get a look at the pop-up shop!"

She'd spent the entire day fidgeting and wishing she was at the pop-up shop. She'd asked her parents if she could call in sick, just this once, so she could be there when it opened. But that had been a big "no." Her mom might be acting supportive, but school would always be first. Not that Emma heard a single thing any of her teachers had said that day anyway.

"Paige texted me first thing this morning and said the press thing last night was a big hit," she told Holly as they rushed toward the front door. "But she didn't give many details."

"We'll see it for ourselves soon." Holly pointed to the school lobby just ahead. "There's Charlie."

It only took the three friends ten minutes to walk to the pop-up shop, which was located just a few blocks from their school on the first floor of an old industrial building that had once been an art gallery. A sign out front featured the *Madison* logo and the title *Choice New Designers' Showcase*.

"That's you!" Holly squealed as they waited to cross the street. "Emma, you're a choice new designer!"

"Not so loud." Charlie tried to stick his hand over her mouth, though Holly giggled and pushed him away. "Allegra here is supposed to be incognito, remember?"

"Oops. Don't worry, I'm over it. I'll play it cool," Holly promised.

Emma stepped off the curb. "Come on," she said.

When they entered the shop, Emma wasn't sure where to look first. The large, high-ceilinged space had been divided into several sections, each decorated in a different color and style to indicate the different designers. Emma's gaze went immediately to her section, which was located halfway down the left-hand side of the room.

The cement wall had been painted the pale blue of a

winter sky, and the headless mannequins were arranged into active poses: one running playfully, one stretched upward holding a fuchsia helium balloon, another walking an invisible dog on a stiff leather leash. A large sign at the front of the section held the Allegra Biscotti name and logo, while a smaller one painted in bright-blue script letters read *Young at Heart*. Tons of people were wandering around looking at the clothes, both there and in the other designers' sections.

"Wow!" Holly hurried forward and spun in a circle, trying to take in everything at once. "This is really cool!"

Emma just nodded. She gazed up at the nearest mannequin. It was dressed in the smock-front dress based on Holly's old birthday favorite. The dress looked larger than life and impossibly fabulous, just as she'd imagined it when it had been nothing more than a few pencil lines sketched onto a sheet of heavy white paper. Were these really her clothes on display for the whole world to see? Could this really be happening to *her*?

CHAPTER 17

NOT-SO-READY-TO-WEAR

Ooh, check out this one!" a woman who looked to be in her early thirties pushed past Emma without noticing her. Her gaze was fixed on the babydoll dress and leggings. Her friend, a stylish redhead in knee-high crinkled leather boots, followed and nodded.

"Nice," she said. "You know, Chloe, you could wear it to the launch party next month."

"Definitely," Chloe agreed. "That would get me noticed if anything could!"

The women didn't even glance at Emma, Holly, or Charlie. Emma traded a glance with her friends. They were both grinning. She smiled back, bursting with happiness. People liked her designs! They actually wanted to buy them and wear them!

"There she is! Emma! Emma!" a familiar voice cried from across the room.

Emma glanced over and saw her mother

waving vigorously at her. Her father was with her. Both of them hurried over, beaming from ear to ear.

"Cookie, we're so proud of you!" her father exclaimed.

Her mother gave her a hug. "You worked hard, and the results show," she said. "Everyone has just been raving about how beautiful your clothes are."

"Keep your voice down." Noah shot an anxious look around. "We've got to keep a lid on the parental pride thing in public."

"Oh, whatever." Emma's mom rolled her eyes.

Emma giggled. "No, he's right, Mom," she said. "You can tell me how wonderful I am as loudly as you like when we get home. For now, hush." She glanced around. "Where is Paige, anyway? I should probably say hi."

"Last I noticed, she was over by the section with the dark-red background wall," her mother replied.

"I see her." Charlie pointed. "Follow me."

Paige and Francesca stood near a black metal mannequin dressed in a red leather catsuit. Francesca was chatting in Italian with a hopelessly stylish and slickly handsome young man in a gorgeous, ridiculously soft cashmere tweed jacket. Emma wondered if he was one of her fellow designers.

Meanwhile, Paige spotted her. "You're here," she said. She looked stunning in a moss-green wool skirt suit and pointy-toed slingbacks. "What do you think?"

"It's amazing," Emma replied. "People seem to like Allegra's clothes."

"You're not kidding." Paige smiled, looking pleased. "The reaction's been stupendous. This could be just the splash of publicity it takes to really launch Allegra's line."

"Do you really think so?" Emma said.

Before Paige could reply, a tiny, bald man in what appeared to be a flowing burgundy silk robe and black silk pants rushed toward them. "Paige, my darling!" he exclaimed loudly. "Another fabulous affair. And the fête last evening was to die for!"

Paige turned to greet him, and Emma moved away and rejoined her friends. "Come on," Holly said, grabbing Emma's hand. "Let's wander around and eavesdrop on people raving about you."

Emma smiled. "Sounds like a plan."

She, Holly, and Charlie headed back toward her section. Her parents had disappeared somewhere into the growing crowd, and within seconds Emma couldn't see Paige or Francesca anymore either.

"Wow, a lot of people come to these fashion things, huh?"

Charlie said as he got elbowed aside by a woman making a beeline for one of the other designers' sections.

"Isn't it cool?" Emma replied. "I—"

Whatever she'd been about to say next died in her throat. The crowd had just parted, revealing a young woman standing in front of the princess dress. She stared up at the mannequin, a puzzled frown on her face.

"Oh, man, it's Nidhi!" Emma whispered in a panic. "I forgot she said she was coming."

"Who?" Holly turned to stare.

"Who's Ninny?" Charlie asked, his voice way too loud.

Nidhi turned her head and spotted Emma. Emma froze, staring back at her. Right away she knew that Nidhi knew.

Nidhi didn't need a paint-by-numbers set to complete the picture. She'd recognized the distinctive fabrics that "Allegra Biscotti" used in her collection. *All* of them.

"Emma," Nidhi said, walking over. A little more dressed up than usual in tall leather boots, a wine-red tube dress, and gold-filigree chandelier earrings, she looked as beautiful as ever.

"I suddenly had a strange feeling that I might see you here, yeah?"

"H-hi," Emma stammered.

"Hey, guys!" A girl bounded over, as if they were all best friends.

"Hi, Val," Holly replied, clueing Emma in that the girl was friends with Jen and Rylan.

"You're Allegra's interns, right? Jen told me. So is she here?" The tiny girl stood on the toes of her shearling-lined boots and peered over their shoulders. "I'm dying to see who's making Rylan's dress."

Emma cast a desperate look at Nidhi. *Please don't call me out,* she pleaded silently. *Not here. Not now.*

Nidhi looked perplexed but said nothing.

"Um, no," Emma told Val, though her gaze stayed locked on Nidhi. "She's not here."

"She got held up in Europe," Charlie added. "You can check it out on her blog. Total bummer, but she told us to take lots of pictures and send them to her." He pulled his cell phone out of his pocket and started snapping photos.

"That's too bad." Val looked disappointed. "Oh well, love the clothes anyway. Bye, Holly." She stepped toward the next outfit, pulling out her own phone to take a picture.

Nidhi reached over and touched Emma lightly on the arm. "Sorry to interrupt, cutie, but I've got to go," she said. "It was good to see you, though. We'll have to catch up next time you stop into the store. *Really catch up.* In the meantime, have fun tonight, yeah?" She winked, then turned and walked toward the door.

Emma felt herself go limp as Nidhi disappeared into the crowd.

"Who was that?" Holly asked. "I liked her jacket."

"She works at Allure," Emma said quietly. "She's kind of a friend."

"Kind of?" Charlie asked.

"No, *definitely* a friend. An even better one than I realized, actually."

An hour later, the pop-up shop was still hopping. Emma's parents had left, but she, Charlie, and Holly stayed to enjoy the atmosphere. Emma was sure she'd never get tired of watching people ooh and aah over her clothes. She was so proud, and it was an awesome feeling.

Nidhi's jacket

"I could really get used to this," she whispered to Holly as the two of them watched an older woman in a charcoal gray, chalk-stripe fitted suit with piles of pearls around her neck wander off after spending a good ten minutes in front of the smock-front dress. She tapped notes into a handheld computer and snapped digital photos. Paige had casually walked by to whisper that the woman was a reporter for the city's most important fashion daily. Emma crossed her fingers that the reporter liked what she saw.

Charlie hurried over. "You'll never guess who just walked in."

Emma followed his gaze. Rylan entered the shop, trailed by Jen and a few more of the see-and-be-seen high-school girls. Emma stood behind a column and tracked them as they wandered about, making loud comments about their favorite clothes and designers. Then they reached the Allegra Biscotti section.

"No wonder you wanted Allegra to design your Sweet Sixteen dress, Rylan!" one of the girls exclaimed.

"Yeah. I can't wait to see it tomorrow night," Jen added.

The first girl nodded. "I almost wish I didn't already have a dress for the party," she said. "Because I'd look amazing in this one." She reached out and caressed the hem of the smock dress. "It's super-adorable!"

Jen headed over to a sleek black kimono dress in the next designer's section. She was so focused on the clothes that she'd passed within a few feet of her sister, Emma, and Charlie without noticing them. "This one's hot!" she said. "What do you think? Is it me?"

"Totally," the first girl said. The girls followed Jen into the other section.

All except Rylan. She hung back in Allegra's section, staring up at the black and sapphire party dress with a look Emma couldn't quite place.

With a jolt, Emma realized it was the dress she'd originally planned to make for her. Did Rylan recognize it from the sketches? Or was she just thinking about how different it was from the dress she was going to have to wear tomorrow night? Emma felt her heart break a little as she watched the older girl. "Let's go say hi," she said impulsively.

She reached Rylan just as Rylan's friends wandered back to find her. "Um, hi, Rylan," Emma said, suddenly self-conscious beneath the curious gazes of the other high-schoolers. Aside from Jen, she doubted that any of them had any idea who she was or why in the world she was talking to Rylan.

Rylan turned and blinked at her. "Oh, hi," she said. "I should've known you'd be here." She glanced over to include Charlie in her comment.

"Come on, Ry," Jen complained. She shot Holly a sour look, as if irritated by her younger sister's very existence. "Are we going to stand around here making small talk, or are we going to shop?"

"Chill, Jen," Rylan ordered. "I'm just saying hi, okay?" She glanced at Emma again. "You're still coming tomorrow night, right?"

"Um, yeah," Emma said. "Thanks. I mean, we'll be there."

Rylan nodded, looked one last time at her almost-party dress, and then turned away. "Come on," she told her friends. "I'm over this place. Let's go get some lattes or something."

She walked out of the shop, never checking to make sure

her friends were following. They were, of course, though Emma heard Jen muttering to one of the others about how moody Rylan was today.

But Emma wasn't concerned about that. She just stared after Rylan.

Holly glanced over at her. "What's wrong?"

"I'm just still not sure I did the right thing," Emma said with a sigh.

"You heard Paige," Charlie reminded her. "She told you like fifty times that you had to do what Mama Sinclare said."

"Yeah. But maybe Paige isn't always right. She also made me swear not to tell anyone about Allegra." Emma caught Holly's eye. "And that was kind of a disaster, at least as far as one particular person was concerned."

"But that worked out in the end," Holly assured her.

"I know." Emma smiled at her. Then her gaze drifted back to the doorway. Rylan had already disappeared, but Emma kept staring that way anyway, replaying what she'd just seen. "But still…Should I have fought harder to get Rylan the dress she really wanted? Or at least a compromise, like the version with the ribbons? It just doesn't seem right that she's going to be upset with her party dress at her own party. I want people to be happy in my clothes."

"Not much you can do about it now, so why worry?" Charlie said.

"I guess." Emma bit her lip and started to turn away from the doorway. But out of the corner of her eye, she saw a familiar figure tentatively enter the shop. Not Rylan this time. It was…Jackson!

Charlie noticed him, too. "What's *he* doing here?" he said. "I never took that guy for the red-hot catwalk type. Maybe he's looking for the gym and got lost."

Meanwhile Holly's blue eyes had gone round and excited. "Maybe you'd better go give him directions to the gym then, Em," she said, giving her a shove.

Emma gulped. What *was* Jackson doing here? Only one way to find out…

She willed herself to walk toward him slowly. She didn't want to seem too excited. He saw her coming and lifted one hand in a casual wave.

"Hi," she said, finding it a little hard to breathe.

"Hey," he greeted her with that cute little half-smile of his. He tossed his hair out of his face and looked around. "Wow, this place is wild."

"Yeah, I guess." Emma paused, not sure what else to say. "Um, are you looking for Lexie?" she blurted out. "Because I don't think she's been here."

Jackson cleared his throat, suddenly uncomfortable but

sort of intense at the same time. "Um, actually, Lexie and I broke up," he said. "We, uh, didn't really have that much in common." He shrugged. "You know."

Whoa! Now Emma *really* didn't know what to say. "Oh," she replied carefully. "That's…too bad."

"I guess. Sort of." Jackson half-smiled and shifted his weight from foot to foot.

Emma waited, but he stood there silent. "So why are you—?" she started, not sure exactly how to complete the sentence.

"I heard your friend Holly telling Lexie about this thing this morning, and I figured you might be here, so…"

His voice trailed off. Emma held her breath. It seemed as if he wanted to say something else. Had he actually come here looking for her? Why? Suddenly the answer to that question seemed more important than anything else in the world.

"Emma!" Paige raced toward her. "Thank goodness you're still here!"

"Um, what?" Emma said. Jackson took a step backward.

Paige didn't seem to notice him there. She inserted herself between them, grabbing Emma by the shoulder. "Some grubby little rug rat just yanked on the hem of one of the dresses and loosened the lining. I need you to come tack it in place, pronto."

"Later," Jackson mumbled.

"Wait! I'll be back in a sec," Emma called to him as Paige

dragged her away, though she wasn't sure he heard her over the din of the crowd all around them.

By the time Emma finished fixing the dress, he was nowhere in sight.

"So this is what trendy hotels look like, huh?" Charlie titled his head up at the polished gray-stone skyscraper they were approaching. "*Tres* fancy."

"Your accent could use some work," Holly teased.

Emma didn't say a word. She was too nervous. It was seven thirty on Saturday night, half an hour before the party was to start. Rylan had texted Emma earlier that day, asking her to come a little earlier to help accessorize the dress.

"Rylan said we should go right in and ask for her," Emma told her friends. She checked her watch. "Francesca's supposed to meet us here soon."

Holly hugged her black wool coat closer around her as a chilly breeze whipped down the street. The skirt of her magenta taffeta dress stuck out beneath the coat and danced in the wind.

"What are we waiting for, then?" she said. "Let's go. It's freezing out here!" She shivered dramatically.

Inside the modern, elegant lobby, a sleek-haired young man in a midnight-blue suit glided toward them. "Sinclare affair?" he inquired with a touch of a French accent.

Emma could see Charlie racking his brain for the perfect witty response. "Yes, that's right," she said quickly before he could come up with one. "Thanks."

"Up the stairs and down the hall to the ballroom," the man said, pointing. "You can check your coats up there."

Soon Emma and her friends were peeling off their coats and scarves and handing them to a checker stationed in the carpeted hallway outside the ballroom. Emma had spent the day redesigning one of her childhood dresses—a tiny flowered-print smock dress—into a mini smock dress and cutting up an old chambray blue shirt of her Dad's to add the panels just as she'd done for Holly's dress. She looked over at Charlie, who was dapper in jeans, a black sports jacket, and a daringly bright plum-colored dress shirt.

Emma let out a low gasp when they stepped into the party space. An enormous room was awash in ecru and seafoam fabric, decorations, and tiny lights. Intricate centerpieces made of huge, puffy white flowers intertwined with what seemed to be artichokes and cauliflower. To top it off, more than two dozen large, round tables were covered in the pale pea-green linens.

"This must have cost a fortune," Emma said.

"But it's so strange," Holly whispered.

"And ugly," Charlie added.

A dance floor with several platforms covered the far side of the room. The DJ tested a bunch of flashing strobe lights. A solitary white light illuminated a life-sized ice sculpture in the center of the room.

"Is that supposed to be Rylan lounging on top of the number sixteen?" Holly asked, peering at it.

"I think so." Emma took in the haughty tilt of the sculpture's narrow chin. Ice queen, indeed! "Do you think that was her idea or her mother's?"

Charlie snorted with laughter. "I bet they both agreed on that one," he said. "The whole ice sculpture thing is just tacky enough for Mama Sinclare, but the ego trip of seeing herself immortalized in ice is right up Rylan's alley."

"I don't know if *immortalized* is the right word," Emma pointed out. "I mean, how long does an ice sculpture last, anyway?"

Holly wriggled her shoulders to the beat as the DJ tested his equipment, adjusting the levels as a lively dance song blasted out of enormous speakers.

"Okay, we might be the youngest people here and all, but this could actually be fun," she said, casting an eager glance at the dance floor, which was currently empty except for a penguin-suited waiter hurrying across it shouldering a tray of canapés and a few wandering high-school friends of Rylan's who'd also scored early admission. It was too dim for Emma to identify any of them for sure.

"It's not time to party yet. We need to find Rylan," Emma reminded her friends. "She said she'd be in her dressing room. Where do you think that is?"

"I don't know. But there's your sister, Holly." Charlie pointed to one of the wandering high-schoolers. "Let's ask her."

Holly smirked. "Yes, let's. Jen's annoyed that I'm even invited to this thing. I'd love to let her know I'm actually here!"

Jen barely looked in Holly's direction when she pointed to a doorway on the far side of the room.

"Rylan's in there," she said. "But enter at your own risk. She's super-cranky."

"Uh-oh," Emma muttered to her friends as they left Jen and hurried toward the dressing room. They knocked on the door and let themselves in. Charlie hung back until the girls declared everyone was decent.

The dressing room wasn't much larger than a closet. It had a full-length mirror on one wall with a small folding table and chair in front of it. As Emma entered, Rylan was taking a sip from a tall plastic cup of soda. Val and another girl huddled nearby. They looked kind of nervous.

"Um, hi?" Emma said uncertainly.

Rylan glanced back. "Well?" she demanded, waving a hand at the plain, subtly ruffled dress. "Any ideas to make this look better?"

Emma's heart twisted. The dress looked…just boring. Rylan's shoulders seemed too narrow because of the scoop neck, and she had no real waist because that's what the sash would have done for her.

But it was when she looked at Rylan's unhappy face that Emma felt the worst. *How could I have done this to her?* Emma couldn't stand it. I have to figure out a way to help her.

But it was too late. *Way* too late.

Wasn't it?

Suddenly Marjorie's voice floated into her mind: *All you can do is be true to yourself, trust your instincts, and let the rest fall into place.*

Emma hadn't really understood what Marjorie meant at the time. But now, instantly, she was pretty sure she did. And she realized it meant she couldn't go through with this. This just wasn't the dress Rylan should be wearing on a night like this, and Emma—*Allegra*—couldn't stand by and let bad fashion happen.

And just like that, she knew what to do.

The plan popped into her head almost fully formed. It was wild and crazy, but then again, so was Charlie's wacky plan to sneak into the gym locker, and that one had worked out pretty well. Maybe this one would, too, if she had the guts to pull it off.

Not giving herself a chance to overthink it, she made her move. Darting past Rylan, she grabbed the tall plastic cup sitting on the makeup table. Then she turned—and threw the soda all over the front of Rylan's dress!

CHAPTER 18

THE LITTLE HACK DRESS

"A re you insane? What'd you do that for?" Rylan shrieked, frantically brushing the splotch of soda. But it was no use. The dress was soaked in sticky brown liquid. "It's bad enough I have to wear this hideous dress—did you *really* just make it even worse?"

Holly and Charlie stood motionless, wide-eyed, both of them frozen in shock. At that moment, the dressing-room door flew open and Francesca hurried in.

"*Ciao, bellas!*" she sang out cheerfully. Then she spotted the soda-stained dress, and her eyes widened. "*Diavolo!*" she exclaimed. "What has happened here?"

"Your little intern friend just ruined my life," Rylan snarled, pointing at Emma. "Even more than your boss already ruined it, that is! And it's too late even to send someone up to my apartment for something else to wear. I'm supposed to make my grand entrance in like twenty minutes!"

Francesca clucked and rushed to her. "Let me see if I might help," she said, grabbing a cotton ball off the table and dabbing at the stain.

"Don't! There's nail polish on that! Oh my gosh, you're just making it worse!" one of Rylan's friends exclaimed.

"*Cribbio!*" Francesca cried in dismay.

Emma took a deep breath…then smiled. "Relax, everyone," she said. "It's all under control. Trust me, okay?"

Rylan didn't seem to hear. She was cursing at Francesca, telling her to get out of her way as she searched the makeup table for something that might help.

Emma pointed at Charlie. "Do me a favor," she said. "Run outside and hail a cab. Keep it there until I join you, okay?"

Charlie only hesitated for a split second. "You got it." He took off through the door.

Emma smiled. She'd been sure she could count on him to go with it. Charlie was like that.

Emma hesitated. Should she just give Rylan her dress to wear? It was pretty cute.

But no. This night was supposed to be perfect for Rylan, and Emma's quickly constructed dress wasn't right for her either. Sure, it would be better than the soda-stained monstrosity Rylan had on right now, but not perfect. Also, Emma was a lot shorter than Rylan. Luckily, though, Emma knew where she could find the perfect dress.

"I'll be back in about fifteen minutes," she told Rylan. "I promise."

But Rylan didn't even look up. She stared at her reflection, seeming to be in shock.

"Don't let her leave this room, okay?" Emma told Holly.

"Wait! What's going on?" Holly demanded.

"There's no time to explain, but I'm going to fix this."

"But how—"

"Just go along with this. Please."

Holly stared at her, doubt in her eyes. Emma held her gaze, hoping she'd earned back enough of Holly's trust.

"Go," Holly told her and smiled.

"Thanks, Holls." Emma dashed out of the room.

She didn't bother to stop for her coat—there was no time. She dashed through the cold air and dove into the cab Charlie had waiting at the curb. "Where to?" the cabby asked, glancing at her in the rearview mirror.

"SoHo," she said breathlessly, giving the address of the pop-up shop. The cabby nodded and swung out in front of a delivery truck, eliciting a loud horn blast. Charlie shot Emma a curious look from the seat beside her.

"What do you have in mind, exactly?" he asked.

"You'll see."

He smiled. "Interesting. Always nice to toss a high-fructose beverage at the party girl. Makes for a memorable event. Something to tell the grandkids about. But, hey, I'll play along, as long as you promise not to soak me next."

Lower Manhattan traffic was a nightmare as usual, but the cabby was a kamikaze. While Emma didn't dare to look out the window for most of the ride, she was relieved when they made it to the pop-up shop in one piece. The place was lit up, but most of the press people had left at this hour of the evening.

"Wait here," Emma told Charlie and the cab driver. "I'll be back in a sec."

She raced inside. Paige stood near the center of the room, watching the last few stragglers. She looked exhausted—and startled to see Emma running toward her.

"What are you doing here? I thought you'd be at the Sweet Sixteen party."

"There's no time to explain," Emma said breathlessly. "But I need Rylan's dress. The real one."

"What? Hold on a second, Emma," Paige began.

But Emma was already rushing over to the sapphire and black dress she'd originally planned to make for Rylan. One or two people gave her strange looks, but nobody interfered as she quickly but carefully unzipped the dress and slid it off the mannequin.

"You cannot take that." Paige's voice was a full octave higher. Emma could tell she was struggling not to shriek in front of the remaining fashion writers.

"I need it. Seriously. I promise I'll get it back here first thing in the morning."

"Where are you taking—"

"Thanks!" she called to Paige, slinging the dress over her arm and sprinting for the exit. "I'll text you later and explain."

The ballroom was packed with fashionably dressed adults nibbling passed hors d'oeuvres when Emma got back. Most of Rylan's friends were crammed in the corner by the DJ. Loud music with a heavy bass line filled the room, and some kids were already dancing. Others were sampling the food or shouting for the birthday girl. Emma noticed Mrs. Sinclare, in a dull oyster-colored dress, standing at one end of the room beside a distinguished-looking man in a suit and coordinating seafoam-green tie.

Charlie spotted them, too. "That must be Daddy Rylan,"

he panted into Emma's ear. "Guess he's back from his business trip."

"Yeah." Emma gulped. Somehow she'd managed to forget that Rylan's parents would be here. It was definitely too late to worry about that now. Keeping her head down, she dashed across the dance floor, dodging flailing arms and tossing heads.

"Okay, everybody!" the DJ yelled into the microphone. "It's time to get this party started!"

The crowd let out a roar of approval. "Ry-lan! Ry-lan!" a few kids chanted.

Emma sprinted to the dressing room. Leaving Charlie guarding the door outside, she let herself in. Rylan sat crumpled on the edge of the chair, her head in her hands. Francesca and Holly stood on one side, Rylan's friends on the other. All of them seemed to be trying to comfort her, though it didn't appear to be doing much good.

Rylan looked up as Emma skidded to a stop in front of her. "Here!" Emma panted, tossing the dress to her. "This is the dress Allegra wanted you to wear in the first place."

Rylan's eyes widened as she held up the dress. "It's amazing!" She jumped to her feet. "Hold this," she ordered, handing the new dress to Holly.

She shoved one of her friends out of the way, kicked off her shoes, and shimmied out of the stained dress. Then, she grabbed the new dress back from Holly and slid it on.

Holly zipped her up and slowly turned Rylan toward the mirror.

"Are you ready?" Emma asked.

Rylan smiled.

"Yeah," she said, looking her reflection up and down. "I'm ready."

"You look like a superstar, Ry," Val spoke up. "And it fits you like a glove."

"Almost," Emma agreed, digging into her purse for pins. "It's a little big in the waist, but I should be able to fix that. Hold still."

After a nip and a tuck, the dress fit as if it had been made to order. Which it sort of had, Emma thought, as she stepped back and looked it over.

"This is more like it." Rylan beamed. "It's beyond perfect! It's exactly the dress I had in mind when I saw that blog. So gorgeous!" She turned toward Emma. "I can't believe you spilled that soda. I never thought you had it in you. Totally inspired!" She grabbed Emma in a tight hug. "Thank you!"

"You're welcome," Emma said, startled. She hugged her back tentatively. "From me *and* Allegra."

She smiled at Rylan, realizing that there really was a genuine person in there. Who knew? Maybe Rylan's snooty exterior had something to do with those three perfect robot sisters of hers or her overbearing mother. Either way, it was too bad Rylan thought she had to act like someone else for the rest of the world.

But then again, Emma also knew a little about acting like two different people…

There was a knock on the door, and Charlie stuck his head in. "Everything okay in here?" he asked, stepping inside. "The birthday girl is being beckoned."

Charlie opened the door wide so they could all see the crowd shouting for their guest of honor. Rylan examined her reflection in the mirror one more time. "Mother's going to have a stroke when she sees me," she said happily. "Serves her right for being such a…such a…" She paused, obviously searching for the right word.

"A harridan?" Charlie supplied helpfully.

Rylan and her friends looked at him in surprise.

"Charlie's, like, Mr. Vocabulary," Holly told them.

"What's a harridan?" Rylan asked him.

Charlie looked surprised. Most people ignored his interesting word choices.

"It's pretty much the same as, like, a shrew. A mean old vicious nag of a woman," he explained.

"Why not just say that, then?" Val murmured.

But Rylan was grinning. "A harridan," she said, as if trying out the sound on her own tongue. "Yeah, I like that."

Emma felt a knot in her belly as she pictured Mrs. Sinclare's reaction. She glanced at the crumpled-up dress lying forgotten on the dressing-room floor. The dress Rylan was wearing now was the complete opposite in every way.

"Are you sure you're okay with this?" she asked Rylan. "Your mom—"

"Don't worry, I won't let her blame Allegra or Paige or you guys either," Rylan promised, sounding much more like her old, supremely confident self. "I'll tell her it was all me. This time and also with the first ruined dress."

Emma's jaw dropped, and then she smiled. "Cool," she said, thinking of the fired maid. One more hint that maybe Rylan wasn't as self-centered and shallow as Emma had always thought. Not quite, anyway. She still couldn't quite forget that ice sculpture out front!

Rylan grabbed a tube of berry lip gloss from the table, slicking it on. "I should have stood up to that harridan"—she shot Charlie a quick grin in the mirror— "as soon as she started taking over *my* birthday party." Rylan capped the lip gloss, tossed it back on the table, and smacked her lips together. "Besides, Daddy just got back from his latest business trip, and he *adores* seeing me in blue. It's his favorite color. I'll make sure he's on my side."

Emma hoped Rylan was right. Either way, Emma realized it was better this way. At least now Rylan could go out there with her head held high.

Val peeked out the door. "They're really yelling now, Ry," she said.

"Come on, girls." Rylan lifted her chin and swept out the door to a loud roar from the crowd as the DJ announced the birthday girl. Her friends followed.

"Oh, how exciting this is!" Francesca exclaimed, rushing out after them.

Emma peeked out the door, wanting to see the reaction to the dress. When Rylan hit the edge of the dance floor, a spotlight picked her up, making the lustrous fabric glisten. Emma smiled.

Then she noticed somebody nearby who *wasn't* smiling. Mrs. Sinclare's eyes had just gone wide and her jaw was dropped. But then about a million camera flashes went off; a bunch of friends rushed forward to surround Rylan; and Emma lost sight of Mrs. Sinclare.

The music started pumping again, and Charlie's limbs started jerking like he was a puppet on a string. "Come on, let's get out there," he said. "I need to get my groove on!"

"Whoo-hoo!" Holly cried, boogying behind him out the dressing-room door.

Emma was about to follow when her phone buzzed. She wondered if it was Paige.

It wasn't. But she didn't recognize the number.

Hi, wutz up? the text read.

Who is this? she typed back.

Jackson.

Emma felt a shiver run down her spine. She stared at his name until it started to blur.

Her phone buzzed again.

From world history class.

She laughed. Oh, wow. He actually thought she didn't know who he was!

She could hear Rylan's laughter floating over the backbeat of the music. She had taken a risk tonight. A big one. And for someone who never took risks, it felt pretty great. Emma fiddled with her phone. She was ready for another.

Want 2 go 2 catch a movie tmorrow?

She held her breath, not daring to breathe until he replied. If he replied. She counted silently to herself. 1...2...3...4...

Ok. Cya.

Emma smiled and then tucked away the phone. It was time to dance.